BLADES OF HAVOC *book two*

pivot POINT

EVA CHANCE & HARLOW KING

Pivot Point

Book 2 in the Blades of Havoc series

All rights reserved. This book or any portion thereof may not be reproduced or used in any manner without the express written permission of the author, except for the use of brief quotations in a book review.

This is a work of fiction. Any resemblance to actual persons, living or dead, or actual events is purely coincidental.

First Digital Edition, 2023

Cover design: The Pretty Little Design Co.

Ebook ISBN: 978-1-998752-25-6

Paperback ISBN: 978-1-998752-26-3

ONE

Luciana

THE BLADES of my skates clicked against the ice as I stepped onto it. With a soft hiss of steel against the frozen surface, I glided toward the center of the rink next to my partner.

I'd imagined what this moment would feel like my entire life.

I'd always thought—always been *told*—that entering any kind of competition was out of my reach. I'd been stifled, kept in the dark when it came to my true skill.

I'd been lied to, manipulated, and emotionally beaten down by the people I should have been able to trust most.

But today made all that anguish worth it.

Today, I would let out the truth of who I was—who I was meant to be. I would fly free in front of an audience, if only for a few minutes.

I wanted to cement this memory into my brain. After all, it was my first competition since I'd started skating fourteen years ago.

I'd only get this moment once.

And no creepy stalker was going to ruin it for me, no matter how hard they tried.

I couldn't stop my gaze from flicking toward the stands with a nervous twitch. Watching for a tell-tale flash of blood red, as if the psycho who'd been haunting me might have left one of his bloody presents here in Dellville's rink, two hours from the town where he'd been harassing me before.

He *could* be here among the decent-sized crowd that'd gathered to see the full competition after yesterday's qualifying round. I didn't really know anything about the creep who'd left dead animals in my bedroom and on my car, who'd taunted me with a doll hung by a noose.

My gut clenched at the memory. I couldn't imagine many *other* figure skaters had to worry about a psychopath while they got into position for their first ever official competitive performance.

Was he already planning his next moves? How far would he take his sick game next time?

I closed my eyes for a second, gathering myself. I couldn't think about that asshole right now.

I had to focus on the men who were standing with me rather than against me.

Jasper caught my gaze, and a small smile touched his lips. The arena lights shone off the pale planes of my partner's stunning face beneath his shaggy auburn hair.

He let out a shaky breath that maybe he thought I wouldn't notice.

A lot was riding on this moment for him too. Jasper St. Pierre, once known as Saint Jasper by his many avid fans, hadn't competed since he'd been sunk by a major slump more than a year ago.

This could be his comeback—or a nail in the coffin formed by his uncertainties.

Our not-entirely-official coach, Niko Okabe, gripped the top of the boards where he was standing by the edge of the rink. At my glance, he shot me a broad smile, but I suspected there was a little anxiety in his twinkling brown eyes too.

He'd come all the way from Japan to dedicate himself to pulling Jasper out of his slump. And I'd discovered that he was invested both professionally and personally, with feelings that were warmer than friendly.

As he swiped his slender hand through his smooth black hair with its stripe of neon pink, my attention slid higher in the stands just for an instant.

I couldn't see my bodyguard, but I knew with every fiber of my being that Rafael was standing up there, watching over me. Silent, unseen, but ready to leap to my defense at a moment's notice.

We'd get through this, the four of us, together. Even if my two fellow skaters had no idea just how much I had to worry about.

I was starting to live my dream, and in the end, that was the only thing that mattered. I had to keep my focus, not just for my men, but for myself.

For five-year-old Lou who'd fallen in love with skating

at a random ice show that her mother had taken her to out of boredom.

For ten-year-old Lou who'd practiced for hours each day after school, determined to do better, to *be* better.

For fifteen-year-old Lou, who'd already seen and been forced to participate in so many horrors, who only found solace on the ice.

Skating had been my only source of peace for so long, the one place where I could experience something beautiful and graceful. I couldn't let this chance slip through my fingers.

"You ready, Punk?" Jasper murmured as we struck our poses, giving his nickname for me a teasing lilt.

"As I'll ever be."

I found that I was actually telling the truth. All anxiety had fled my heart. I was left with nothing but quiet resolve.

The moment the familiar melody began to play over the speakers, my heart started to pound. On the third beat, we pushed off across the ice in graceful synchronization.

Our measured breaths became one, our heartbeats thudding along in the same rhythm. Confidence wrapped around me like a warm blanket, more than I'd felt performing the same routine yesterday, even if there were more onlookers this time.

Jasper and I would do our best. I knew every move, every spin, lift, and jump, and I simply had to show it.

It seemed that Jasper felt the same way. I caught his expression: the gentle, expressive smile that curved his full lips up.

Even as we swept into our first sequence, I had to marvel at his grace. He was all broad shoulders and powerful limbs; it didn't seem like he would be able to glide across the ice with so much elegance, but he seemed more at home on the rink than off it.

We spun, jumped, and landed together to spiral around each other. I imagined a trail of color, sparkling silver and gold flowing behind me as I swayed in time to the music.

Jasper and I swiveled toward each other. At the music's highest trill, my hands found his. Our arms twined together, necks tilting, backs arching.

The melody swelled, the sweeping arrangement filling both my ears and my heart. I barely felt myself land the next jump.

There was nothing in me or around me but the resounding symphony and the beauty of our routine. My heart soared along with every note, every spin, every pose.

No matter what any psycho stalker did, no way could I ever give this feeling up.

We breezed through the first lift without even the slightest hint of a quake in my skating partner's arms or my own stance. I'd been so caught up in the joy of the routine itself that I'd had no time to worry about whether we would struggle.

I swung through the air, perched on Jasper's palm, without a care in the world. The routine felt as natural as breathing.

When he lowered me back down to the ice, I reveled in the power and strength contained in his brawny arms.

We shot into our synchronized double Lutz without

hesitation, our bodies twisting midair simultaneously. This routine had followed me into my dreams, replaying over and over like a tape stuck on repeat, but one that I could watch for eternity without getting tired of it.

I backpedaled until I was flying in reverse, my dark ponytail whipping around my face. These were the moments I lived for.

My heartbeat quickened as I circled back around, facing my skating partner. We were coming up on the lift that had always been hardest for us.

If we could just pull that off, then I could believe we'd really see this through to the end as the entire routine was meant to be.

Resolution shone in Jasper's eyes as he glided forward. His hands reached for me, and I leaned into his hold, giving over my trust to my partner.

He lifted me up, higher and higher until I was truly soaring now. His powerful arms supported the pose I struck with a surge of strength that made my body crave his touch even more.

One rotation.

Two.

A third time, each whirling motion perfectly in time with the music.

As he lowered me, my arms swept outward. I landed soft as a dove feather.

We'd done it. We'd *nailed* it.

A grin stretched across my face. My body careened through the last part of the routine as if floating on joy.

Jasper caught my hand and held it up in our final pose. Even if the power had gone out right then and there, my partner's bright smile would have been enough to light the room.

And he aimed it right at me.

A whoop I knew was Niko's carried from the boards. A pang ran through my heart at the connection I felt to both of these men who'd come together to build my dream with me.

With the last note of the song fading, a moment of silence gripped the arena. My pulse only had the chance to stutter with concern once before a thunder of applause broke out through the stands.

I looked up at them, watching rows of spectators stand as they brought their hands together. So many more smiles beamed down at me. One old man in the front hastily wiped away a tear with the back of his glove.

My grin stretched even wider, happiness surging up inside me as if it would carry me all the way to the ceiling.

Was the sicko who'd been harassing me watching up there too? Let him.

I was a force to be reckoned with. I hadn't let my mother destroy my life, and I sure as hell wasn't going to let any psycho stranger do it either.

And this was only the beginning.

TWO

Luciana

WAITING for our scores felt like the longest few minutes of my life. We'd gone last, so the number the judges were calculating would determine exactly where we placed in the rankings.

The thing was done. We could sit back and celebrate the fact that we'd made it through the routine so flawlessly, no matter how we did in the actual competition itself. Nerves or not, I wanted to savor this moment for all it was worth.

And it was worth the world to me.

My hands wound tightly together as I rested them in my lap, my butt freezing from the chilled metal bench. Beside me, Jasper's knee jiggled up and down in his anxiety.

Niko, though, was as still as a cat who had spotted a

mouse, his bright brown eyes on the judges as they marked down our scores. My eyes flicked over to the announcer as another employee handed him a sheet of paper.

Oh, Lord. Here it comes.

My stomach lifted as though I were about to go hurtling down a roller coaster's steep first drop. The announcer adjusted his glasses and squinted down at whatever was written there.

"And the score for our final pair is… fifty-two point three-nine! That puts them in first place."

First place.

Those two words beat around in my skull, echoing like a shout into a cave. Jasper and Niko let out a joint cheer.

The crowd was whooping and clapping, but I could barely even hear them. I was frozen, stunned by what we'd just accomplished.

With this being our first routine as a pair and there not being much time to prepare for the small local competition, we hadn't included the most complex moves that could have made an even higher score possible. I'd already calculated the maximum we could possibly achieve with the jumps and lifts we were going to perform, and we'd come just a couple of points shy of total perfection.

A grin broke across my face, and I spun toward Jasper to wrap my arms around him. He laughed and hugged me back.

This was real. We'd not just competed but *won*.

As I let go of Jasper, Niko grabbed me in an embrace of his own. "I hope that puts all those doubts your old coach gave you out of your head."

A choked giggle sputtered out of me. "I guess it has to."

Had Coach Balakin ever imagined I'd be capable of this? Would he have been surprised or sad because he'd always known he was holding me back under my mother's orders?

Niko pulled back and beamed at the two of us. "I only wish you could have seen your routine from the stands. It was breathtaking. Just stunning. I got it on video, but that won't compare at all to the experience you just gave these people. Congratulations!"

"Congratulations to you, too," Jasper said, nudging Niko's shoe with his. His smile was sunnier than I'd ever seen it. "You're the one that got us here."

"We won." I breathed out in a giddy rush. "We... we really did it!"

"Yeah, we did." Jasper grinned. "We showed this competition what we're made of, huh?"

All of our hard work and all of that effort had actually paid off. My years of training under Coach Balakin had done a lot of good, even if he'd never admitted how much.

The man might have been forced to lie to me about my skill, he'd still done his best for me, had tried to give me everything he gave his other normal students whose parents didn't happen to be leaders of a vast criminal organization.

And he'd died for his efforts.

Tears blossomed in the corners of my eyes. I didn't wipe them away in time for Niko and Jasper not to notice.

"Lou, you alright?" Jasper asked, his voice low. "If you want to go somewhere quiet—"

"No, no." I brushed a hand across my face, reining in the swell of grief that had momentarily overwhelmed my hammering heart. "It's just that… I don't know, I thought this moment would never come. I didn't think I would ever get to feel this way—not once in my whole life. I just can't believe we pulled it off!"

My eyes traveled up to the stands; I knew that somewhere, Rafael was watching me with pride glowing in his burgundy eyes. I only wished that he could be down here with me now, and then my heart would truly be full and complete.

For now, though, it was enough to know that he was here, that he had seen my routine. That he had seen me finally win.

The announcer had just finished reading out the names of the winners—mine with the fake last name I'd had Niko register me under—calling us onto the ice. Jasper and I made our way down to the center of the rink again.

Our winnings weren't much: two fifty-dollar gift cards for local caterics, two more to the sporting goods store in between here and Hobb Creek, and a small metal trophy in the image of an ice skate. You couldn't expect much more than that from a competition this low-key.

But I didn't need grand prizes to revel in the moment. I gripped Jasper's hand as we grinned like fools in the center of the rink, clutching our gift cards and our cheap trophies.

Jasper grabbed my hand as we returned to the stands to a little more fanfare. "We should probably go get changed, huh? Meet you in the front hall after? We should go out to celebrate."

"You bet." I squeezed his hand hard before letting go.

We snatched our equipment bags and made our way to the locker rooms, Niko following at our heels. He nodded to us, still smiling as bright as the afternoon sun outside.

"I'll be right here."

Jasper pushed the door to the men's locker room open. "Let's go somewhere that's serving breakfast for dinner. I'm dying for some waffles."

"Of course you are," I called after him with a snicker, and headed into the women's locker room, my thoughts spinning in my head in a joyful daze.

This is so surreal.

The dream-like feel of the moment only increased with the various skaters who offered their congratulations as we changed side by side. I smiled and thanked them and complimented their performances even when I couldn't remember the routine, my hands whipping through the motions.

I just wanted to get back out there and see my men again. My lessons with Coach Balakin had always been solo, so I wasn't used to this community vibe, as nice as I imagined it could be once I got used to it.

These other women were my peers, not people who I had to gaze at from afar, wishing I could be one of them. Not anymore.

I wriggled out of my skating costume and pulled on my faded black skull tee and pinstriped leggings before slipping my clunky rings that could serve as weapons as well onto my fingers. I only took a moment to glance at myself in the mirror.

Okay, I had to admit I'd earned Jasper's nickname.

Despite my haste, my partner was already waiting for me in the hallway, Niko beside him. The sight of them together, happy and relaxed, was enough to make my heart sing.

Even in the artificial arena lights, I didn't think I'd ever found them more striking—or irresistible.

My heart thumped faster, and so did my steps as I closed the gap between us in urgent strides.

Jasper's eyes gleamed as he took me in. "Lou, we—"

I didn't give him the chance to finish his sentence. I snatched them both by one arm and dragged them around the nearest corner, away from the locker rooms and the distant murmurs of the exiting audience.

The only thing I wanted was to feel their bodies against mine, to taste victory on their lips.

The moment that I was sure we were alone, I thrust myself into Jasper's arms and kissed him. He hesitated for only a split-second before he pulled me closer, his lips parting against mine.

He tasted like fire and ice all at once, steaming hot in desire and chilled from the rink. I nibbled on his bottom lip briefly, then teased his tongue with my own.

His hands moved up into my hair, his fingers mussing my ponytail. He let out a tiny gasp that tickled me somewhere low in my belly, his eyes darkening when he pulled away to meet my gaze.

Now *that* was a victory kiss.

"You were really amazing out there," he said, his voice gone rough. "So fucking beautiful."

As my cheeks flushed at the emphatic compliment, he glanced over at our coach. I caught a flicker of uncertainty in his expression before he squared his shoulders and stepped closer to the other man.

"And you've been amazing too."

Jasper leaned in to quickly press his lips to Niko's. It was something softer and more cautious than the embrace we'd just shared, but the sweetness of the gesture was palpable.

A different sort of joy swept through me as he eased back with a cautious smile. My lovers were finally working through their own crap to find their way back to where they'd started.

Niko blinked at Jasper and then grinned, at least as pleased as he was startled. "I'll accept the compliment and the gift that came with it. But I can't leave my favorite girl out."

He flashed that impish grin at me before pulling me in for a kiss as well. I smiled against his lips, a giggle bubbling up in my throat.

I loved the playful part of him so much. His lively personality had become a source of comfort to me.

My two skaters contrasted with each other, but together they made something more special than I could have ever imagined being possible back in Austin.

And then there was Rafael now, too.

My good spirits dampened just slightly at the memory of my bodyguard's confession—and the brief makeout session we'd had last night. I was going to have to tell

Niko and Jasper that my relationship with the other man was shifting in a new direction.

They'd known I wasn't exclusive, but I'd explicitly told them that he was just a friend. I didn't want them thinking I'd lied about that.

Although we shouldn't get into all the things I *had* lied about, or at least avoided telling the truth about. I hadn't even competed under my real name.

My gut knotted. My past had to stay in the past. It was safer for all of us that way.

But I was going to be honest with them about Rafael.

We'd need to go somewhere more private for that conversation. I wasn't going to get into my complicated love life when any of the other skaters could come around the corner in the middle of my explanation.

Maybe at dinner we could get a cozy booth in a not-too-busy restaurant that would give us the space we needed. Or I'd invite them over to the bungalow after. Niko hadn't even seen my house before.

I tugged at both men. "Come on, let's go get that dinner. I'm starving."

We made our way back out to the main hall, still grinning like shy middle schoolers who had just shared their first kiss. A few of the other skaters were still standing around chatting, adding to the community vibe I was just starting to appreciate.

Someday I'd really fit in with the rest of them.

We'd almost reached the lobby when a trill of a voice called out from behind us. "Jasper St. Pierre! Oh, and your lovely partner is with you too. What luck."

All three of us turned to see a middle-aged woman

making her way down the hall toward us, waving for our attention with just the tips of her fingers. The thudding of her clunky high heels echoed through the hall. Her startlingly bright blue eyeshadow should have clashed with her sunflower-print dress, but somehow the contrast gave her a quirky poise.

"Oh, I'm so glad to have caught you." the woman said. "It was so wonderful to see you performing again, Jasper. That performance was absolutely moving."

Jasper peered at the woman with a hint of confusion before he pasted on a smile in an even more impressive performance than he'd given on the ice. I could tell that he didn't actually recognize her, and he probably wanted to tell her to buzz off, but he knew better than to let his usual grumpy self show in front of a fan.

"Thank you," he said, tucking his hands behind his back. "I'm glad that you thought so. Creating a visual that's emotionally compelling is always my main goal."

The woman laughed like a crow with something caught in its throat. "And you do it so well." She turned to me. "And I don't believe we've met, but you rose to Jasper's level quite spectacularly. I can't wait to see more from you."

Feeling a little out of my depth, I didn't know what to say other than a repeat of Jasper's "Thank you."

She arched her eyebrows at me. "And I do expect to see more of you. Will you be competing for Canada or coming down to join us at U.S. Figure Skating?"

I opened my mouth and closed it again, and latched on to an appropriate diversion. "You work for the association."

"Oh, yes, look at me not introducing myself. I'm Martha Maderline. I'm not high enough that it'll do you much good to butter me up, I warn you, but I can still tell you how much we'd love to have you on board."

Understanding dawned in Jasper's eyes as he must have remembered seeing her before.

I couldn't help asking, "What are you doing all the way up here in Dellville?"

Maderline gave her croaking laugh again. "I heard from a local friend that Jasper was performing again and I just had to take a quick jaunt up here to see it for myself. And imagine my surprise when I saw who was coaching you! Niko Okabe, what an unexpected delight."

"Yes," Niko said with obvious amusement. "It's a little far from my usual territory. But you don't get the chance to coach a talent like Jasper St. Pierre every day. And Lou, too. She's a big up-and-comer, you know."

"I could see that with my own eyes." The woman patted my arm so fondly that I found myself warming to her despite her overblown personality. "Congratulations on holding your own with big names like these two. You're really going somewhere, I'm sure of it."

This time my smile came with a little uncertainty. "That means a lot to me."

Maderline set her hands on her ample hips. "Well, I'll let you get on with the celebration I'm sure you're planning after that win. I just had to say hello, and also to *insist* that you come compete in the qualifying series if you're at all inclined to return to Jasper's home country. You still have a week to sign up before the cut-off. Don't miss it!"

Jasper rubbed the back of his neck. "We'll certainly think about it. Thank you again."

She waggled her fingers at us once more and sashayed out into the parking lot. A giggle bubbled in my chest, but a prickle of nerves held it in place.

Jasper glanced at Niko. "She really thinks I'm back at that level again?" There was no mistaking the hope in his voice.

Niko snorted. "Of course you're at that level. You'd breeze through the qualifying competitions, as long as you don't get in your own way." He prodded me with a teasing finger. "Both of you would."

A softer smile curved Jasper's lips, but one that looked totally genuine. "Maybe we *should* give it a go. The way I felt on the ice today… It was almost like it used to be. Or better, just a little different than I'm used to."

He aimed his smile at me, and my pulse fluttered. Getting such an eager vote of support from someone who worked for the national skating organization was huge— and it lit me up inside seeing Jasper acting more sure of himself.

"I guess it could be worth trying."

"Worth trying?" Jasper gave my ponytail a tug of mock-consternation as we stepped out into the warm late-afternoon sunlight washing over the parking lot. "You should be chomping at the bit for this, Punk. Place high enough in the early competitions, and we could be at Nationals in a few months."

It should have made my heart soar to see him talk about that possibility with nothing but happiness. Instead, a chill trickled through my veins.

If we started competing at larger competitions, especially south of the border, the chances that my mom would catch wind of my location would increase exponentially. I knew from my own figure-skating viewing that the qualifying competitions were mostly broadcast on specialized channels that people who moved in her circles weren't likely to be tuning in to.

But Nationals? That'd be shown on any station with significant sports coverage.

Coach Balakin's sallow, lifeless face flashed behind my eyes, and I had to restrain a shudder.

Every step further I took on this journey toward my dream, I put the two men with me in more danger. Danger they couldn't possibly anticipate.

But how could I tell them that we should stay here and stick to tiny local competitions? How could I drop out of my partnership with Jasper when he'd just started finding his way out of his slump?

Nausea congealed in my gut, but I knew there was only one answer.

I was going to have to come clean. Tell them the whole story of who I was and where I'd come from.

And then I'd find out whether they even still wanted me around, let alone competing with them.

THREE

Luciana

I WISHED I could have appreciated my introduction to Niko's apartment more. The four of us tramped up the stairs next to a cute thrift store and stepped into a bachelor pad lit by the last rays of the sinking sun through its broad front windows.

I could tell that during the day, the whole place would be as bright as Niko's attitude. His personal touch to the place was minimal, probably because he hadn't been able to bring a whole lot of possessions over from Japan with him, and the space had a tidy feel. But his presence showed in the postcards pinned to the fridge with magnets and the collection of weights and other training equipment next to the futon.

It even smelled like him, warm and tart. I should have been loving this moment.

Instead, my stomach had twisted into one big knot.

Rafael glanced at me with a questioning expression. On the drive over, he'd asked me if I was sure I really wanted to do this.

"You know I have to," I'd told him. "If I leave Niko and Jasper in the dark with the danger I'd be putting them in, I'd be *worse* than Mom."

Rafael had grimaced. "We don't know how they'll react. They could panic and do something… unwise."

I'd rolled my eyes at him. "I don't think they're going to call the cops on me. And if it looks like they might, we'll just have to disappear again."

Better that than I got the two men I'd started falling for killed by dragging them into the line of fire unaware.

Niko smiled as he swept his arm toward the cozy space, but his expression was curious too. At the end of the dinner which I hadn't been able to enjoy all that much either, I'd told him and Jasper that there was something important I needed to talk to them about and suggested we go back to one of their places.

I didn't trust the bungalow, not really. Not when my stalker had already targeted it more than once.

Jasper wasn't one to beat around the bush out of politeness. He turned to face me and folded his arms over his chest.

"So? What's the big important news?"

"It's not exactly *news*…" My throat constricted.

I dragged in a breath and sank down on Niko's couch. My heart hammered at my ribs.

I'd only just found real happiness here in Hobb Creek with these two men. Was I going to lose it already?

Would the admiration and affection I'd treasured in their eyes fade away into disgust and horror?

But I did have to tell them. Maybe I should never have hidden it this long to begin with.

I swallowed thickly and looked up at the three men. Rafael moved to stand by the arm of the futon beside me.

His brow furrowing, Jasper gripped the back of the boxy armchair. "Is everything okay?"

Niko settled onto the futon next to me and gave my knee a quick but reassuring squeeze. "Let's give our angel a moment to work through her thoughts. If you need anything, just say so, Lou."

He was being so sweet about it that I winced inwardly. I was even less of an angel than I'd ever claimed to be.

I set my hands on my lap, where they twisted together awkwardly. "The thing is, there's something you should know before we decide about competing on a larger scale. I—I haven't told you the whole truth about how I grew up."

Niko frowned with obvious concern. "You mentioned that you had a hard life at home. We didn't need the details."

"You do, though. Because... the *reason* it was a hard childhood is that my mother is the ruler of a major criminal organization. Like, think the mafia, but with even more influence and power."

Jasper's eyebrows shot up. "You ran away from the *mafia*?"

I shook my head. "Not even the mafia. Listen. It's— she's—even worse. She commands legions of underlings and has control over business all around the world, and she's not afraid to kill. And she expected me to become just like her."

Silence fell over the room. It pressed down on me as if a sack had been pulled over my head, but I forced myself to push on. I had to get it all out.

"That wasn't—that wasn't what I wanted to be. *Who* I wanted to be. I've always wanted to skate. I never lied about that. But she… I think she paid off my coach to tell me I wasn't good enough, to make sure I never thought I should be competing or going anywhere with it. And then, when she thought I was old enough that I should be taking more responsibilities as her heir…"

A shiver ran through me with the memory of Balakin's corpse, the blood-stained ice, the knowledge that he'd died because of me.

Just like these two men might if Mom ever found me.

"What happened, Lou?" Niko asked, quietly but gently.

I stared at my clenched hands. "She had my coach murdered. Left him for me to find. Acted as if it was a good thing because I could finally move on in the direction she wanted."

Jasper sucked in a ragged breath. "Holy shit."

"Yeah," I said, fighting down my nausea. "That was when I knew I couldn't stay any longer. I grabbed what I could and took off—and Rafael insisted on coming too. He's been my bodyguard for years. I needed to find someplace she'd never think to look for me and, well, we ended up in Hobb Creek. You basically know the rest of that story."

Rafael's gaze slid from one man to the other, his

expression grim. "She's felt guilty about not telling you everything, even though she didn't owe it to you. Even now, she could have cut and run rather than getting into it. Remember that."

Jasper rubbed his hand over his face and blinked at me. "That just sounds crazy. Why *are* you telling us now?"

He wasn't recoiling in disgust, which I guessed was a win. But now I had to get into the hardest part.

"My mom will be searching for me. If she figures out where I am, I don't know what she'll do, but you could become targets. I'm already getting harassed by a stalker who could be connected to her somehow—we don't even know."

I lifted my gaze to meet Jasper's and then Niko's eyes. "She might kill you if she realizes I've been skating with you, like she did to my old coach. The more publicity we get, the bigger events we compete in, the higher the chance is that she'll catch on and you'll be in danger. I don't want that to happen. And I totally understand if you don't want anything at all to do with me now. I didn't mean to get your hopes up under false pretenses."

Niko leaned toward me, searching my face. "How much danger are *you* in, Lou? You said someone's already been bothering you?"

Really? After everything I'd just told him, he was worried about *me*?

"I don't know," I said. "Some sicko has left dead animals around my house and things like that, but I have no idea who's doing it. But it just proves that I'm a magnet for trouble."

Jasper snorted. "Well, we already knew that, Punk."

The joke came out a little strained, and his smile was stiff around the edges. But he looked at me steadily.

"There was always something that sounded a little strange about your story," he added. "This whole thing *is* crazy, but somehow I don't even feel that surprised. It's not okay that anyone's messing with you, doing psycho shit like that. If you need to crash somewhere else for a while—"

"You're welcome to stay here, as long as you need," Niko jumped in before Jasper could make the offer it'd seemed he was leading up to.

I gaped at both of them. "Are you listening to me? Your lives could be on the line. I'll do whatever I can to make sure she doesn't discover what I'm doing and to keep you safe if she does, but it's a huge risk, no matter how you slice it. A risk I can't ask you to take."

Jasper flexed his shoulders, a scowl crossing his face. "I'm not going to run away and let you take all the heat on your own."

Rafael cleared his throat and aimed a glower at the younger guy. "I can look after Lou just fine."

Oh, shit, if they weren't kicking me to the curb, I still had to explain about my evolving relationship with my no-longer-just-a-bodyguard too.

Were my skater men really taking my confession in stride? I studied both of them again, afraid to let myself get relieved just yet. Not sure I even should be relieved.

"You'd really want to stick with me? Both of you? I don't know how—Jasper needs to get out there and compete in bigger events—I don't want to hold him back."

"We'll figure something out," Jasper said without hesitation. "You deserve to be out there in the spotlight too."

He cut his gaze to Niko, who nodded emphatically. "We aren't going to abandon you, Lou. We're a team." He glanced up at Rafael. "All of us."

I swiped my hand across my mouth. "Um, if that's the case, then about the whole team thing… I should probably also tell you that while Rafael and I *weren't* anything more than friends when I introduced him to you, it seems like that may be changing."

As both of the other guys' attention zeroed in on the man standing next to me, Rafael drew himself even straighter, his expression as impenetrable as usual.

"That doesn't mean I don't want the two of you too," I added hastily. "The way I feel about all of you… Maybe it's selfish. But there's something there, something special even if it's different with each of you. Again, it's up to you what you do with that information. I just felt I should keep being honest with you about seeing other people."

To my shock, Niko broke into a laugh. "Well, when you have all that history with him, and he cared enough to stay with you even after you ran away—honestly, I was surprised when it sounded like there was nothing more going on."

He caught Jasper's gaze, and some wordless communication appeared to pass between them. I resisted the urge to fidget as another silence fell over us. Of course they needed a little time to process everything.

"I can go," I said. "If you want to talk about it just the two of you, or—"

Jasper shook his head and sat down in the armchair. "I don't think that'll be necessary. We *are* a team, we're in this together, and we're going to get out there on the ice again. No more-than-a-mafia mom is going to get in your way."

As Niko nodded, hope flooded my chest. I couldn't judge how well they understood what they were really getting into, but I'd told them everything I could. From the firmness of Jasper's tone, he was taking the situation seriously.

Niko rubbed his chin. "The qualifying series competitions aren't very widely publicized. I doubt they're the type of thing most gangsters would be watching."

"That's true," Jasper said. "I don't think it'd be all that much risk giving one of those a go. We could pick somewhere you don't think your mom has connections— there are a bunch of the qualifiers all over the country. And if we get farther than that, into events that are broadcast more widely, we could change up your appearance so you're less recognizable in general."

From his intense expression, he was already imagining disguises he could design like he did his skating costumes.

I stared at them, my words shocked out of me. They were willing to risk so much just to keep me in their lives.

I hadn't let myself give up, but deep down, I'd been sure they'd walk away. That the truth about my past would be too much for them.

Instead they were committing themselves even more than they had before.

Jasper took in my face and grimaced. "Don't look like that. Of course you shouldn't have to give up your dream

—not for your mom or any crazy stalker. I just wish we could have done more to protect you sooner."

Niko raised his chin, any playfulness vanishing. "Well, now that we know, we can be better prepared. We won't let your stalker win, whatever they're after. Rafael, you're just going to have to get used to Jasper and I looking out for Lou as well."

I half expected my bodyguard to argue, but instead he let out a low chuckle. "I guess I can't complain about sharing the workload. But you have to take this seriously. These people mean business. It's like nothing you'll ever have dealt with before."

"Then we'll learn," Niko said. "That's always been a part of this job."

The rush of joy and affection overwhelmed me. I scooted over to pull him into a hug and then moved to the armchair to embrace Jasper as well.

He hugged me back tightly. "We've got you, Punk. No matter what they throw at you."

"Thank you," I mumbled.

My spirits were soaring... but a thread of doubt remained coiled around my gut.

If they didn't fully comprehend what they were signing up for by throwing their lot in with me, would I really be able to protect *them*?

FOUR

Niko

I STUFFED my last few shirts into my second suitcase, unable to stop myself from hearing my father's voice in the back of my head, chiding me for not being more careful to avoid wrinkles. As if a few creases in my clothes were worth worrying about right now.

Every time I slowed down in my packing, I saw Lou's face as she'd made her confession to us. The anguish in her expression and her voice replayed in my head.

I should have been rejoicing that the skater I'd come around the world to coach had regained his confidence enough to want to enter the next round of official competitions. And I was thrilled that Jasper had agreed. But I couldn't help worrying about the other pupil I'd ended up taking on.

Whatever exactly Lou had been through in her

childhood, she hadn't deserved it. I'd seen how compassionate and generous she was.

She lived on beauty and grace. And her family had tried to drag her down into grime and violence.

I had no experience dealing with organized crime directly. We all heard stories, of course—of the yakuza back home, of the "mob" in America—but I could admit I wasn't sure how to protect her.

I only knew I was determined to do it one way or another.

Cursing my past self for insisting on bringing so much with me from Japan, I lugged the two suitcases and my equipment bag down to the car I'd leased. It'd seemed extravagent when I'd signed the contract, but I'd quickly realized that getting around Canada required a personal vehicle. You couldn't simply hop on a train from Hobb Creek to anywhere.

As I pushed the suitcases into the trunk, my ringtone pealed out from my back pocket. I pulled out my phone and hesitated for a second at the sight of the unknown caller.

But how would any criminal or stalker have gotten *my* phone number?

Shaking my head at myself, I tapped the answer button. "Hello?"

A woman's no-nonsense voice carried from the speaker. "Is this Niko Okabe?"

"Yes, it is. What's this about?"

"Oh, good, I'm glad I reached you. This is Sally Bakers from Whetstone Sporting Goods. You reached out about some talent looking for sponsorships—Jasper St. Pierre and a Luna Garcia?"

My spirits lifted even with my momentary jolt of confusion. Right, I'd registered Lou for the qualifying competitions and submitted her and Jasper for possible sponsorships using the fake name from one of the assortment of passports she'd turned out to own. We'd gone with the Luna one because it meant she could keep the nickname "Lou" without anyone finding it odd.

"Yes, I did. I hope you enjoyed the video of their most recent performance."

"We were *very* impressed with what we saw. I'm prepared to offer you a sponsorship for the two of them. Especially if they're going to be competing at larger scale events... That is the case, isn't it, Mr. Okabe?"

"Absolutely." I shut the trunk and pulled open the driver's-side door. "Actually, we're on our way to Boston now to prepare for a qualifying competition there before hopefully continuing on to Finals and Nationals."

If anyone pressed further about why we were moving to the United States weeks before the actual competition, I'd have told them that I wanted my skaters to get comfortable in the new setting well ahead of time, even if we couldn't train in the exact same rink where the main competition would be held.

The full truth was that I also wanted to get Lou away from her stalker here in Hobb Creek, and the Boston competition was the one farthest from Austin, where she'd said her mother's organization was based. It also happened to be the site of the Pairs Finals this year, so we'd already be in town if my two skaters accomplished everything I knew they were capable of.

"That's excellent to hear," the store representative said. "I can tell they'll go far. I'll be emailing you the contract and additional details. If you could look it over by the end of the week and get back to me with any questions or concerns, I'd appreciate it."

"Absolutely, Ms. Bakers!"

I'd be reading through that email the second it arrived in my inbox. I hung up with a smile tugging at my lips.

This was definitely good news. Skating was an expensive career at the best of times. With a solid sponsorship, Jasper and Lou wouldn't have to worry about how they'd cover their rink time, equipment, or the materials Jasper would need when he got down to making his fully custom costumes.

There. I might not know how to fight off career criminals, but I could support Lou in plenty of other ways that she needed too.

And if I needed to protect her by facing off against literal threats, I'd do that too. I could stand up for people other than myself.

I was going to do right by her, like the man I'd always intended to be. No slip-ups this time.

There was even more on the line now.

My smile tightening with determination, I dropped into the driver's seat and cruised the short distance to Jasper's apartment. We were going to drive down together while Lou and Rafael took their own car, meeting up for meals and a rest overnight at the halfway point.

As I parked outside the house with its large, detached

garage that held Jasper's temporary home, my thoughts veered in a totally different direction. To the press of his firm lips against mine three days ago at the Dellville arena.

The memory sent a quiver through my veins. My heart thumped a little faster as I stepped out of the car, anticipating seeing his impressive form and handsome face appearing at the top of the stairs outside the apartment's entrance.

I'd known we needed to talk since Lou had insisted on bringing up the subject of our original kiss from almost two years ago. I hadn't wanted to distract Jasper before his first competition in ages, but I didn't have that excuse anymore.

We needed to clear the air. I needed to find out where we stood, what he wanted out of our relationship, even if it was possible I wouldn't like the answer.

Who knew if he was looking back on the kiss as happily as I was?

I bounded up the steps to see if he was finished packing and was just reaching to knock on the door when Jasper opened it. He peered out at me with his eyebrows raised.

"There you are. I thought you were going to make me wait around all day."

I couldn't help laughing. "Me? You're the one I usually have to drag out of this place. I thought you might need help getting organized."

"I can organize just fine. But you might as well come in, since I'm sure you'll want to confirm that."

He'd taken on a typical grouchy tone, but it was light

enough that I knew he wasn't actually in a bad mood. He was just being Jasper.

Grinning, I followed him into the cramped space.

He did already have his own suitcase packed—just the one, as well as a backpack and his equipment bag. Of course, he hadn't come from anywhere near as far away as I had.

I cocked my head as I considered the space. "Do you want to stop at your grandparents' house before we head down south so you can pick up more things?"

Jasper shook his head. "Nah, I have everything I need." He shot me a sideways glance. "You just want to let my Grandma ply you with her butter tarts again."

I held up my hands. "I was only looking out for you. Although if there were certain delicious tarts involved in the visit, I wouldn't complain."

Jasper let out a rough chuckle that did something funny to my stomach. Of its own accord, my gaze lingered on the firm line of his jaw. Then it dropped to the sculpted brawn of his chest under his fitted T-shirt.

Those muscles flexed as he hefted his bags and stepped close to me where I was waiting by the doorway. "If you're satisfied, let's get going."

His scent filled my nose, warm and musky—perfect. It would have been easy to nod and put off the conversation again, but I knew once we were stuck in the confines of the car, I'd feel even more awkward.

I cleared my throat, and Jasper paused, probably sensing the shift in mood.

"I actually—there was something I wanted to talk to you about first."

Jasper knit his brow. He set down his suitcase and studied me. "Sure. What's up?"

I opened my mouth, closed it again, and forced out the words. "We kissed the other day at the arena—that is, of course you know that—and before, after the competition in Munich— Is that something you want? For our relationship to shift in that direction? If you'd rather keep it totally professional, I can. I never expected, just because I came out here…"

As I trailed off, Jasper smiled crookedly. "That's pretty obvious from the fact that you've never brought it up or made a move the entire time you've been here."

I grimaced. "I did try to lead up to the subject a couple of times, but you'd get tense. I didn't want to push."

Jasper ducked his head for a moment. "I don't know. I — You know my head hasn't been in the best place. Maybe I was a little scared if you kept talking about it you'd end up telling me it'd been a mistake. Because I do. Want something like that. With you. Um."

He glanced up at me, his face flushing adorably. I wanted to kiss him again right then.

"I never thought it was a mistake," I said quickly. "Unless it really had thrown off your skating career—but it never was for me."

"Yeah, I guess that should have been obvious from the fact that you traveled halfway around the world to help 'fix' my skating. And just to be clear, that first kiss had nothing to do with my slump. I promise." Jasper's smile grew, smoothing out my jangling nerves. "I don't want to rush into anything. I've never done anything with another guy before. I didn't even know I could be attracted to guys until that night in Munich. But I definitely am—to you. I'd like to see where that could go. If you would too."

I beamed back at him. "Yes. Absolutely. There's no rush."

Seeing his stance relax at those words sent a rush of pure joy through my body. He looked so pleased that I couldn't resist the urge that gripped me next.

I crossed the small space between us and touched his jaw to bring his mouth to mine. Jasper hummed low in his throat, the reverberation passing through the kiss.

So what could I do but kiss him a little harder? I held myself back from jumping into everything I'd imagined doing with this man but reveling in the feel of his lips as they parted against mine. Celebrated the flick of his tongue as he gained enough confidence to flick it briefly into my mouth.

Slow. I could do that. I could move at a snail's pace if it meant Jasper was right here with me like this, figuring things out as we went.

He drew back gently, shooting me an even brighter smile than before. "I guess we'd better swing by Lou's place before she starts thinking we must have gotten lost on the way."

I grabbed one of his bags to help him carry them out. "Can't leave our woman waiting."

The bubble of warmth that seemed to surround us as we tramped over to the car left my heart singing. But at the same time, a darker thread wound through my chest.

I needed to defend this relationship with all I had too. It was on me to make sure I didn't screw things up.

FIVE

Luciana

THE CHILLED air rushed through my ponytail, my skates gave a soft click as they met the ice, and a song swelled around me. Pure bliss.

The feeling was no different here in Boston than it'd been in Austin or Hobb Creek, even if the arena was a little bigger and fancier. And more crowded.

I veered neatly around a couple of other practicing skaters, timing my movements with the beat of the third song among the options Niko had offered for our free skate. We could use the same routine we'd performed in Dellville for our short program, just increasing the difficulty of a few of the moves to meet the official standards, but we needed a longer one with other specific criteria as well, and that meant we also needed more music.

I skipped up in a tiny bunny hop alongside the melody and laughed when I caught sight of my skating partner's and coach's faces.

"What?" I pumped my legs back towards them as Niko killed the music. "I thought the song was fun. Not sure it's exactly what we'd want to go for with the routine, though. What do you think, partner?"

Jasper tilted his head as he considered. "I usually go for something more emotional rather than upbeat. I did like the second one you put on, Niko. Play that one again?"

"Sure." Niko thumbed through the list on his phone.

The song started right where he'd cut it off before, a little under halfway through. The tune wasn't quite as poignant as the classical piece we'd used for our short program, but the dramatics of the mix of strings, guitar, and drums were definitely enthralling.

It would be a difficult song with its shifts in tempo, but if we could nail it, it would totally be worth it. The impression it would leave on the judges and on the crowd would be overwhelming. I could already picture us whirling across the rink, catching them up in the picture we made.

I pushed off against the ice and kicked my heels up in a waltz jump. My emotions lifted alongside my body.

Yeah, this melody was something I could really skate to.

I circled around another skater seconds before I veered too close, abruptly self-conscious. I wasn't used to sharing the rink with anyone other than Jasper, and even his presence was still new to me.

But Niko had said it'd be good for us to go out during

the freestyle session. We'd get a chance to see some of the other skaters we'd be up against and what they were capable of, their styles and strengths.

Of course, that also meant they were getting a look at *us*.

Ignoring the prickling over my skin brought by other skaters' gazes—real or imagined—I glided back to Niko and Jasper as the song ended. They were standing closer together than I'd ever seen them, their shoulders nearly brushing. There was an ease to their closeness that lit me up from the inside.

They'd obviously started to figure out whatever was happening between them. Good for Jasper, going for that kiss in Dellville. I hoped Niko had finally opened up about his feelings too.

"This song is definitely the best," I announced when I reached them. "Let's be ambitious. You only live once, right?"

Jasper snorted, but he also reached out to tug my ponytail affectionately. "Spoken like a punk, Punk."

Niko grinned with a faraway expression. "You two could create something spectacular with this. And I know exactly where we'd want to include some of the jumps already."

He pulled out his notepad and started scrawling his thoughts out in kanji. His primary language helped ensure no one else would be able to steal his inspiration, although I wished I could read it myself.

I craned my neck to scan the music app on Niko's phone. "You've got a huge collection of playlists there. Are they all for skating?"

"Oh, they're for everything." Niko slid his phone back into his pocket. "Cleaning, shopping, eating…"

"You have a playlist for eating?" Jasper arched an eyebrow up at him.

"You don't?"

As the two of them fell into a light-hearted debate about the importance of background music, I watched the rest of the skaters do their thing. One of the other women landed a triple Axel before my eyes, sweeping across the ice like it was nothing.

I clamped my jaw to stop it from dropping. Jasper and I weren't casual skaters either—I'd pulled off triple Axels before—but this was my first real official foray into the professional scene. I wasn't used to being surrounded by this level of skill.

These were skaters who had likely competed over and over, who had already been able to show the world what they could do. They would have backers and fans and maybe were even a few favorites of the judges. And I was going to go up against them?

But when I looked at Niko and Jasper again, none of that mattered. I had the two of them and Rafael watching over me from somewhere in the shadows at the back of the stands, my safety always on the forefront of his mind.

This was a new start for all of us. If everything had gone according to plan, my stalker had been left to eat our dust back in Hobb Creek. We were moving on to bigger and better things.

There was an entire world here just waiting for us to crack it open like a golden egg.

A cocky voice with a hint of a rasp broke through my

reverie. "Look who's here. Jasper St. Pierre finally shows his face again?"

I whirled on my skates to see a man who probably wasn't more than a year or two older than my nineteen propping his arms against the boards a few feet away. The arena lights glinted off his golden-blond hair, slicked back from his forehead without a strand out of place. He was dressed like a skater—long-sleeved thermal and gloves—and his wiry frame held plenty of lean muscle to support that assumption.

And really, what else would he be doing here? He definitely wasn't old enough to be coaching.

Jasper's shoulders tensed as he turned to meet the stranger's piercing blue eyes. This guy obviously wasn't a stranger to *him*.

"You're training here too?" he said with an unmistakable edge in his voice.

The new guy shrugged and straightened up, pulling at his gloves. "It's the best option in town. Or maybe you forgot after all that time away. How long has it been since you last showed your face at a rink? A decade or so?"

His arrogant tone had me bristling in an instant. If any of the guys back home had talked to me or someone I cared about like that, they'd have been getting a knuckle sandwich.

But this wasn't back home; this was a professional skating venue. I had to deal with the jerks here a little more politely.

Something about his looks struck a chord of recognition in me: hard-edged but handsome with his smooth, pale skin broken by a faint scar that ran up his chin to his lower lip. I probably *should* know this guy.

Jasper glowered at him. "I needed a break."

The other guy guffawed. "Sure. A break from knowing your time in the spotlight was limited with all the new talent coming up. The nerves could get to anyone."

I stepped forward, narrowing my eyes. "Funny, I'm not seeing a whole lot of talent from you so far—other than for shooting your mouth off. Maybe you're talking about yourself."

The blond guy's gaze darted from Jasper to me, startled and then sparking with vicious amusement. "Who the hell are you? Jasper's coach brought on some fresh meat so he'd look better in comparison?"

My teeth gritted, but Jasper touched my shoulder in a gesture that felt like a warning. He fixed the jerk with a glare.

"This is Lou, my *partner*. And you wouldn't be talking shit like that if you'd seen her." He turned to me. "Quentin Wolfe. Sorry you had to meet him."

His terse but dry tone got a laugh out of me.

Quentin Wolfe—I did recognize that name. He'd made his mark in the Juniors competitions that I'd sometimes watched when there wasn't enough new higher profile stuff to study. He'd gotten onto the national team last year, though he'd been one of the less prominent members.

Quentin let out a low chuckle of his own. "Your partner? You're skating *pairs*, St. Pierre? I guess you figured that way you wouldn't have to go head-to-head with me."

"Hard as it may be for you to believe, I haven't given

you much thought at all," Jasper retorted, but his jaw was tight.

"You're going to find it hard to ignore me now. I look forward to watching you crash and burn all over again, old-timer."

Quentin tossed aside his skate guards and pushed off across the ice without giving either of us a chance to respond.

I rolled my eyes at his retreating back. "Old-timer? Who inflated his head so big?"

When I turned back to Jasper, my partner was scowling. "He's a fucking prick. Better to ignore him."

I took in the storm clouds that'd gathered in Jasper's gray-green eyes, and my stomach knotted. "Is he like that with everyone?"

"Probably. But he's worse with me." Jasper sighed. "When he first transitioned from Juniors, the media liked to pit us against each other in their coverage because we were close in age and our styles are so different. He took that as his cue to make my life hell. It figures he'd be training here."

"You have nothing to worry about," Niko piped up. "The last time you were competing against Quentin, you made it to the international circuit and he was stuck at home."

"Yeah, but last year he made it to Worlds. Which obviously inflated his ego even more." Jasper let out another breath and shook his head. "Whatever. It's true that I don't have to go up against him directly while we're competing in pairs. It's all just hot air anyway."

He didn't sound like he totally believed that, though.

Frowning, I glanced over to where Quentin was going through his initial on-ice warm-up.

It was easy to see the contrast between him and Jasper, even in the basic spins and jumps he was working through right now. My partner was all fluid motion, wrapping you up in the story of his movements.

Quentin angled every limb with perfect precision. His expression stayed locked in analytical intensity, as if he were calculating the exact degrees of every turn, every lift of a leg or arm.

Technically, he hit every mark. There was no denying the power that showed as he whipped through the air.

But even as I admired his overall form, the performance left me cold. It was almost mechanical in its deliberateness, no sign of the artistry I admired so much in Jasper.

I let out a humph. "Even if you were competing with him, he couldn't hold a candle to you."

That got a smile out of my partner, even if it was a strained one. He slung his arm around my shoulders. "Thanks for the vote of confidence."

As he spoke, one of the female skaters glided over to join Quentin where he'd stopped for a moment not far from us.

She tilted her head at a coy angle and batted her eyelashes, thick and dark with mascara. "Hey, Quentin. We ended up at the same arena again. Must be meant to be."

Quentin grinned at her, the expression as sharp as his moves. "I guess I can look forward to my off-ice time now too, Jess." He gave her ass a swift pinch.

Jess let out an exaggerated gasp and then giggled. "You betcha."

She swiveled around to flash a red-lipped sneer at me before soaring off across the rink again. Irritation prickled under my skin.

What the hell was the matter with these assholes?

To my further annoyance, Quentin glanced over right then and caught me watching. He aimed a broad smirk at me that felt like a challenge and shot off after Jess.

I turned my back on them and touched Jasper's cheek. "We'll just ignore him. Both of them."

"That's right," Niko said. "You've got to get used to the competitive atmosphere again."

Jasper let out an inarticulate grumble. "Quentin will definitely get me up to speed in that area fast."

Our coach squeezed his arm. "Focus on your own skills. No one will be mocking you after they see how far you've come. Let's stick to this corner of the rink. I'll play that song again, and we can work out how some potential moves could come together."

As I floated over the ice next to Jasper, I tried to envision an ideal free skate. This was a much bigger deal than the small, amateur competition in Dellville—this was serious.

People were watching.

And not just watching. In between spins and jumps and a few quick lifts that Niko had us run through, my gaze slid to the stands.

Even for this practice, several figures sat on the benches—friends and family members here to encourage the skaters. And a few of them had their phones out, filming the moves.

They'd inadvertently be recording *me* too, here and there.

A shiver ran down my spine that had nothing to do with the chilly air.

I was here under an assumed name. That should have granted me all the anonymity I needed at this level of competition.

But if people posted those videos online—if the wrong person happened to see them…

All it'd take was one bit of bad luck, and my mother would be racing up here to put me in my place. And do who knew what to my men as well.

My throat constricted. The hiss of my blades over the ice suddenly sounded more ominous than exhilarating.

I couldn't let that happen. My men had promised to protect me—and I had to protect them in turn.

I had to do everything in my power to make sure there wasn't the slightest chance the wrong person would see me and think of Luciana Cordova, the Deadly Rose's daughter.

SIX

Luciana

IT TURNED out that applying eyeliner was like riding a bike—once you learned, you didn't forget.

I hadn't bothered with flashy makeup since I'd left Austin—and even back in Austin, I'd stuck to a little mascara and lip balm when I was in mafia princess mode. I'd saved my fun, striking looks for my periodic club nights. Since I hadn't gotten the chance to compete on the ice back then, I'd never done a performance look for my skating sessions.

Even Mom had rarely seen me with cat-eye liner, vibrant shadow, and vivid lips. Her associates wouldn't connect the me I was creating in front of the mirror to the old Luciana Cordova at all.

What would Mom have thought of me now? I could

hear her voice in the back of my head: *Women in our position don't need to paint our faces like clowns.*

She'd been all about keeping it simple and a little severe rather than artsy. But I didn't think I looked anything like a clown.

I turned my head from left to right, assessing myself. The bright green eyeshadow dusting my lids paired with the turquoise in the corners really popped in contrast with the red hue I'd dyed into my dark hair.

I hadn't been sure about the bangs the hair stylist had chopped across my forehead, but as I brushed my fingers through them, I decided they were definitely cute rather than dorky. And they were one more way my appearance was transformed.

Every day, I'd put on this face for our practices. Even if someone who'd known the old me caught a glimpse of a recording, it shouldn't trigger the slightest jolt of recognition.

I blotted the deep red lipstick to tone it down just slightly and gave my reflection a smile. "Right. I think that does it."

I set my new makeup bag in the cabinet alongside Niko's razor and Jasper's aftershave. It was a little weird suddenly living with not one but three men in the three-bedroom apartment we'd been able to find not too far from the arena, but I had to say I loved having easy access to my guys.

Like right now. I pushed open the door to find Niko and Jasper hanging out on the sofa in front of the TV, Jasper flipping channels restlessly. Time for the first trial run of the new look.

I didn't even have to clear my throat to get their attention. Both their heads turned my way at the squeak of the bathroom door.

I couldn't imagine anything much more gratifying than the way their faces lit up at the sight of me. The genuine sign of approval made my heart leap.

Jasper let out a low whistle. "You look amazing. But I hardly recognized you. I guess that's the point, right?"

Niko chuckled. "I almost thought we were being held up by some mysterious, red-headed robber. You're an expert makeup artist as well as skater."

My smile faded a little. "It kind of sucks that I'll be going out there not exactly looking like myself. But it's fun putting it on. And I'll be able to refine the look to go with our costumes once we get those sorted out."

Niko clicked his tongue and leapt up to give my bangs a light ruffling. "Your spirit still shines through. You'll never stop being Lou, no matter what we're giving as your full name."

I laughed, warmed by the affection in his tone. "Thanks for the vote of confidence."

"Speaking of costumes…" Jasper got up with a stretch of his arms and checked his phone. "We'd better get going if we're going to make it to the fabric store with plenty of time to look through the options before closing. Do you want to come along, Lou?"

I shook my head. "Nah. I trust your artistic eye a lot more than my own. I'm sure whatever you pick will look amazing."

And it might not be a bad thing if he got a little one-on-one time with Niko to foster whatever relationship they were growing between them.

Jasper bumped his shoulder against mine. "No pressure, huh?"

"Hey, I've seen what you can do. I have total faith in you."

I bobbed up to give him a quick peck, brushing my lips lightly so I didn't leave an imprint. Niko leaned in to kiss my temple, and the two men headed out together.

"Oh, hey," Jasper said a little awkwardly after he'd opened the door. A second later, Rafael stepped past him with a brusque nod. My bodyguard was just returning from one of his periodic sweeps of the neighborhood.

After the other men had left, Rafael checked the lock and then turned to me, his face showing no reaction to my mask of cosmetics. He'd already seen the new hairdo, watching over me at the salon.

"See anything concerning out on the streets?" I asked.

Rafael was still very much in bodyguard mode. Along with his patrols around the apartment building, he'd insisted that he'd take the sofa at night rather than sharing one of the bedrooms, so that he could be our "first line of defense" against intruders.

His dedication didn't surprise me, but part of me couldn't help hoping he'd warm up to the other men beyond simply tolerating their presence in our lives. Eventually.

He pulled off his jacket and hung it on one of the hooks by the door. "No sign of danger that I could pick up on. I'll do another circuit later tonight."

"So, it seems like we've left my psycho stalker back in Hobb Creek?"

"As far as I can tell." He aimed a faint smile at me, which from Rafael was practically a grin. "He hasn't left any calling cards yet, and I'm not sure how he could have figured out where we are. But I'm not letting down my guard until we're sure."

"Of course you aren't." I grinned back at him and then struck a modelesque pose. "So what do you think of my full disguise?"

His gaze swept over my face, leaving my skin tingling in its wake. There was analytical precision to it, but also a heat in his eyes that he didn't attempt to suppress.

I'd been longing to see that kind of desire in him for so long. It was hard to believe he was finally offering it.

"You know how to pull off an extreme look like that," he said. "You'll be drawing lots of eyes, but I don't see how anyone from the old life will recognize you. I think you look best as yourself, but this is a good shield."

I think you look best as yourself. Had he ever expressed any opinion about my appearance before?

The guys at the clubs had preferred flashy Lou. But Rafael had known me for all the most important parts of my life—and he'd finally decided that he wanted me. No pretenses, just as I was.

He finally recognized the woman I'd become instead of only seeing the girl I'd been.

A flutter passed through my chest, and for a second I lost my words. "Well, I'm glad to have your approval."

The corner of Rafael's mouth quirked upward into

something more like a full smile. "Lou, you know I've never *not* thought you were gorgeous."

The flutter grew into full-out beating wings. I swallowed thickly and tipped my head toward the bathroom.

"I don't really need the disguise right now. Just wanted to try it out. Help me get all this crap off so I can go back to being myself?"

I could have washed up by myself, but I wanted to see if he'd agree. And, okay, I also appreciated the excuse to have him with me in the tighter space.

We stood next to the sink, and I poured out some of the remover onto a cloth. Then I offered it to him and tilted up my face with my eyes closed so he could ensure every trace of shadow and liner was wiped away.

Rafael brushed the damp fabric over my skin so gently my heart skipped a beat. My pulse kept thumping faster, every inch of my body aware of his closeness, the heat of his brawny body.

He set his other hand on the side of my neck, his thumb braced carefully against my jaw while he wiped off the other eye. My breath caught, and he paused.

His voice came out rough. "I'm sorry. Did I hurt you?"

"No," I said, hearing my own voice gone husky. "It's just… nice, having someone take care of me. You've always been good at that."

"Not that you need all that much taking care of anymore," he said dryly. "You're very capable of doing it yourself, as you like to prove on a daily basis."

I wrinkled my nose at his teasing. "Yes, I absolutely

can look after myself. But that doesn't mean I can't enjoy having help."

"Well, you have it. As long as you want me. I can't think of a job I'd rather do than protecting you."

More heat unfurled under my skin. When he lowered the cloth, my eyes slid open.

Rafael met my gaze, both of us unspeaking. I took another cloth to wipe off my mouth and the foundation I'd laid over my forehead, cheeks, and chin. Then I lifted my face again.

"All done?"

"All done."

I set the cloth on the sink and wet my lips. Rafael's gaze tracked the movement. Every nerve in my body was screaming at me to throw myself into his arms.

Instead, I set my hand on his chest. Just testing, to see how he'd respond. The last time—the only time—we'd kissed before, my stalker had interrupted us. I wasn't really sure how to pick up where we'd left off.

His thumb stroked over my cheek, lighting flames in its wake. "Lou…"

"You like me best like this?" I asked, gazing up at him.

There was no mistaking the fire burning in his eyes. "Siempre." *Always.*

"Then why don't you show me just how much you do?"

The words had barely left my lips before he was claiming them with the crash of his mouth into mine.

SEVEN

Rafael

LOU WAS the sweetest thing my tongue had ever tasted. I could never have imagined how addictive her kiss would be, and now I couldn't imagine ever pulling away from her.

She nibbled on my lip with a gentle scrape of her teeth that struck me like a bolt of lightning. I swallowed a groan, not wanting to show how desperate for her I already was.

Instead, I let my fingers run rampant in her newly colored hair. The strands were so soft, so delicate, so fragile.

Something inside me tightened. More than anything in the world, I wanted to make her mine. Dominate her body and soul until every inch of her was quivering with need like I was.

Show her all the passion I'd kept under wraps for so long and how well I could bring it to bear.

As her arms wound around my back, her nails tracing fine lines through the fabric of my shirt down my back, I reined in the impulse. This was still new, whatever we had together. I had to be careful with it.

She might be all woman, but she'd had a crush on me since she was practically a kid. I had to make sure she was totally on board with the change in our relationship every step of the way.

Her tongue darted between my lips again with a playful swipe. I closed my eyes, savoring the sensation for all it was worth.

My hands slid down to stroke over the sleekly muscular planes of her perfect shoulders. Lou hummed encouragingly, the sound setting me on fire.

I kissed her harder with a growl and pulled her tight against me. She *was* mine now. Maybe she had feelings for two other men as well, but in this moment it was just me and her.

I'd accepted her as a woman, and that meant I could enjoy all the benefits that came with it.

But not too forcefully. Not too demanding. Simmer down, Rafael.

She might have left the mafia princess life behind, but she'd always be royalty in my eyes.

As I loosened my hold, Lou dipped her head to plant a trail of kisses along my jaw. Her lips drew a scorching line all the way to my ear.

When she nipped the lobe, I couldn't suppress my groan. My cock twitched within my jeans, achingly hard.

Lou shot me an impish grin before continuing her torturous course down my neck. It was all I could do not to slam her against the wall and grind the proof of my arousal against her pussy until she was pleading for release.

I wasn't going to cede all control over the situation, though. I grabbed her wrists and backed her up until I had her caught against the door. She dragged in a tiny breath, her eyes on mine, but she didn't tug against my hold.

No, the heat in her gorgeous eyes was nothing but welcoming.

She wasn't the only one who could tease. I lowered my head to the crook of her neck and flicked my tongue over the smooth skin there. When I sucked on it, she rocked against me with a gasp.

Fuck, I needed more. I wanted to drown in this woman.

No other lover had ever consumed me like this. It was as if I'd been waiting my whole life to give in to Luciana Cordova.

Catching both her wrists in one hand and keeping them raised over her head, I slipped my other hand beneath the hem of her shirt. My fingers splayed across her toned stomach.

I couldn't resist the swell of her breasts. Without thinking, I jerked at her bra hard enough to snap the band.

As my palm closed over one breast, Lou squirmed against me with a whimper that both inflamed me and made me hesitate. What kind of animal was I going to be here, ripping up her clothes?

But as I forced my touch to gentle, my fingers to

stroke tenderly rather than urgently over her curves, Lou peered up at me through her eyelashes.

"Don't hold back with me, Rafael. I've wanted this for so long. I'm not afraid of you."

I inhaled with a hiss and let my mouth crash down against hers again. As I tweaked her stiffening nipple between my thumb and forefingers, she moaned against my lips and wriggled her hips.

The friction sent a flood of heat through my groin. I hefted her up, balancing her against the door with her legs splayed around my thighs so we could lock together even more fully.

With a yank, her shirt was on the floor. I'd had to release her wrists to accomplish that, and she wound her arms around my neck again, reclaiming my lips.

After she'd ravished me so thoroughly my head was spinning, her fingers groped at my own shirt. She wrenched at the buttons and then heaved the whole thing off so we could press together skin to skin.

The feel of her breasts against my bare chest had my cock throbbing twice as hard. Lou kissed my shoulder and traced her hands down over the ridges of muscle, setting off sparks everywhere she touched.

"I don't think this is how you really want me, is it?" she said coyly, and let her fingers drift lower. She traced the waist of my jeans. "I can tell that a very important part of you is begging for attention."

"I don't beg," I muttered, even though I was the barest of threads away from it when she talked like that.

"No? Hmm, I wonder if I could change that."

She flicked her fingers right over the bulge of my cock,

firmly enough to make me groan but so quickly the sensation passed before I had a chance to enjoy it.

Another growl slipped from my throat. I pushed her against the door with a thrust of my hips, and Lou's head tipped back with a hitch of breath.

A sly smile crossed her lips. "Am I being too much of a brat for you?"

My pulse stuttered. "What?"

"You're making that face—the one you always do when I get up to something you don't totally approve of. Don't lie. You *totally* think I'm a brat sometimes."

"That's not—" I started to argue, and then she skimmed her fingertips over my groin again. My sentence cut off with a growl.

Lou's grin widened, and suddenly my hesitation seemed ridiculous. The connotations of the term obviously didn't bother her. She thought it was funny.

We both knew she was my equal in every possible way. It didn't matter that I had twelve years on her or what labels we put on things.

"You are *definitely* being a brat right now," I said in a low voice, tipping my face close to hers. A twinge of discomfort ran through my chest as I said the word, but it faded at Lou's laugh.

"And what are you going to do about it, old man?" she murmured in a husky tone that went straight to my cock.

How were those words so hot? How did this suddenly feel so *right*?

Because she was owning it. And if she could lean into the parts of our dynamic that I'd once found so worrying, then I could too, couldn't I?

Bracing my hand against her thigh, I whipped her off the door and yanked it open. Another giggle spilled out of her as I strode across the apartment toward her bedroom.

"You're in for it now," I informed her.

"Oh, no." She squirmed in my arms, her pussy brushing my cock. "Whatever shall I do?"

I didn't know whether to snort with amusement or groan with unfulfilled desire.

I pushed into her bedroom, kicked the door shut behind us, and spread her out on the bed with me looming over her. Her dark red hair fanned out around her gorgeous face, a tempting combination of devilish and angelic.

"What are you going to do with me?" she asked, a little breathless.

"I'm going to return a little of the torture."

I ran my hand up her leg and hooked my fingers under the waist of her leggings. They had to go.

And go they did. I slid them down inch by inch, stroking my thumbs in teasing arcs across the skin I bared as I went. Holding Lou's eager gaze every step of the way.

Her eyes glazed with hunger. She wiggled her legs as if to urge me faster, but I held them down and pressed a kiss just above her knees on both sides.

"Rafael," she said, stretching my name out in a mock-whine.

I couldn't restrain my smirk. "Brats get what's coming to them."

"Fuck, yes."

When I reached her ankles, I whipped the leggings the rest of the way off her. Then I drank in her nearly naked form—the perfect curves, the smooth light brown skin marked here and there by paler scars.

Some of those wounds she'd taken in gang fights, others on the ice. Both were a testament to how strong and committed this woman was.

And she was mine.

Lou pushed her elbows behind her and arched her back to emphasize her breasts. "Like what you see?"

"You know I do."

She wet her lips. "I want to hear you say it."

Her tone was all seductress, but the longing in her eyes didn't look like only lust to me. Behind the confident woman, was she still a little scared that I'd shut her down before we took this encounter to its obvious end?

I'd turned her away so many times before. I had to show her that would never happen again.

"You're perfect." I reached for her last remaining piece of clothing, the thin panties clinging to her hips. "There's never been anyone I wanted more. And now I finally have you to myself."

I punctuated each word with a suggestive tug of her panties. In a matter of seconds, they joined her leggings on the floor.

I took Lou's entire body in, wanting to memorize the sight and keep it locked in my memory. Her breasts rose and fell with her giddy breaths. A gleam of arousal shone on her beautiful pussy.

She was ready for me, but I wanted to savor this moment. And I wanted her to as well.

I might not be the only man in her life, but I was

damn well going to make sure she never forgot how good it was with me.

I leaned forward to press kiss after kiss down her stomach. She lay back, enjoying every brush of my lips, every trail of my tongue and nibble of my teeth.

When I came to her pussy, I let my heavy breath rush over her clit. She shivered, her legs shifting farther apart as if in offering.

I finally gave her what we both wanted. I swiped my tongue across her exposed pink nub.

A guttural sound reverberated from Lou's lungs. She pressed up against my mouth, not hesitating at all about encouraging me to keep going.

She tasted like everything I'd ever dreamed of. Her pussy pulsed against my tongue, her thighs grazing my cheeks.

When I inched lower to slide my tongue into her slick slit, I got a chorus of whimpers as my reward. She raised her knees, giving me more room to work.

"Good girl," I murmured, and her fingers stroked over my scalp with another moan.

I circled her clit with my thumb, pressing down on her while I still gave her everything I could with my tongue. I used every ounce of knowledge I'd gained with other women—all the women who'd never meant half as much to me as the one I was pleasing now.

Her hips rose with every delving thrust of my tongue. My thumb swiveled over her tender nub. When her fingers curled into the sheet on either side of us, I knew she was close to her peak.

And I was going to take her all the way there.

I threw myself into eating her pussy with wilder abandon, bringing my lips and the tips of my teeth to the task alongside my tongue. Lou bucked, a cry breaking from her throat.

Then her body stiffened, her pussy clenching around my extended tongue. I suckled her as she rode out the wave of her release with a string of noises that were close to sobs.

As her body went slack, I raised my head—and found myself being shoved back by those slim but powerful arms.

Flushed but grinning, Lou yanked at the fly of my jeans. Before I'd really recovered from the bliss of having her writhing under my mouth, she'd gotten the zipper down and delved her hand inside my boxers.

"Dios mio." At the careful graze of her fingernails around my shaft, my hips swayed toward her of their own accord. "Fuck, Lou."

She wrapped her fingers around me and stroked me from base to head. "I think we both want this in the same place as soon as possible. What are you waiting for, Rafael? Are you going to take me or what?"

I reared up and caught her face in my hands, kissing the satisfied smirk off her face. The brat was definitely asking for it now.

As I jerked off my jeans and boxers, Lou grabbed a foil packet out of her nightstand. I wasn't sure I'd ever seen a sexier sight than her tearing it open with her teeth.

I snatched the condom from her and unrolled it over my straining length. Then I pinned her back down on the mattress.

"Is this what you want?" I rumbled, rubbing the head of my cock over her folds.

She gasped and arched toward me. "Hell, yes. Give me all of it."

I'd meant to tease her longer as payback, but I couldn't resist when she made a request like that.

I pushed into her an inch at a time, knowing I was a big man in every respect. But Lou's pussy was so hot and slick it was like I was meant to fill it.

Before I was even halfway in, she started rocking to urge me onward, and then I was a goner.

I thrust into her, carefully at first and then with increasing speed. Lou ran her fingernails down my back and squeezed my ass, and a groan tore from my lungs.

Any reservations I'd once held had melted completely away as if they'd never existed. Lou had made damn sure of that. All that was left was our desire, melding together and becoming one, just as we were now.

I grunted, giving her everything. My hands splayed against the sides of her head, my fingers digging into the pillow as I pounded into her.

She bucked to meet me just as eagerly, clutching my body to her. I snagged a fistful of her silky hair and pulled.

Her mouth dropped open, her breath coming in hot, heavy gasps as she panted for me. Her dark brown eyes reflected hints of gold as the sun fell across her from the window, her brows lifting high.

"Holy shit," she mumbled. "Rafael, harder... Yes, yes, just like that."

I lifted one of her legs to let me enter her even deeper, and a thrill of pleasure slipped from her lips. Her pussy gripped my cock with the perfect blend of friction and heat.

She jolted beneath me, her eyes closing as our hips slammed together. Her breaths shortened, and her nails dug into my ass with pinpricks of pain that only heightened my desperate pleasure.

My own breaths had become unsteady gasps as well. There was a gauge inside of me that was quickly filling, rising like a thermometer in Death Valley.

"Fuck, I'm close." As I spoke, I felt myself lose a little more of the control I did have. "You feel too goddamn good."

Her response was to wrap her free leg around me, forcing me further inside of her. She'd lost all words now, her lips parted only to pant.

She started to tremble beneath me. My name burst out of her in a gasp, and her pussy clamped tight around me.

I couldn't hold back any longer. A wave of pleasure washed over me with a blazing release of pressure in my balls. I came harder than I ever had before in my life.

I kept bucking into her as I spent myself. Lou clung on to me, her breaths gradually evening out.

Finally, my head drooped over hers. I couldn't quite bring myself to pull out of her yet.

Lou didn't appear to mind. She raised her head for a brief kiss and trailed her fingers over the tattoo on my arm with my brother's name. Her fingertips absently spelled out *Edmundo*.

"That was fucking fantastic," she informed me. "You see, we should have been doing this all along."

I couldn't stop the guffaw that sputtered out of me. "Not *all* along."

She gave me one of those cheeky smiles. "Okay, the last year, anyway."

It hit me then that she might even be right.

I nuzzled the side of her face. "I'll just have to make up for it by getting you off all over the place in all kinds of ways from now on."

Her eyes sparkled. "Is that a promise?"

As I gazed down at her, I realized it wasn't the promise I most wanted to make. I wanted to tell her it could be like this forever—because I'd make sure no asshole gangsters or crazy stalkers got close enough to so much as frighten her ever again.

I only hoped I was strong enough to truly stand beside this incredible woman I'd underestimated for so long.

EIGHT

Luciana

JASPER GLIDED to a stop next to me and rolled his shoulders with a sharp exhalation.

"I know we're technically not done with practice, but I'm going to head to the locker room a few minutes early. Can't quite shake the ache in my back, but the heat from the showers usually does the trick."

That sounded fair enough, especially considering Niko had taken off ten minutes ago for a meeting with another potential sponsor.

I gave Jasper's hand a quick squeeze. "Sure. I'm going to work on that spin a little more on my own, and then I'll be heading out too. I'll see you at the apartment."

Jasper shot me a smile and pushed off toward the stands. As I watched him go, my stomach knotted.

Were his sore muscles only because of the training we'd

been putting in here over the past week, or was it more than that? I couldn't help wondering if his apprehension about tackling this competition with a total newbie coupled with the bomb I'd dropped on him and Niko about my past were catching up with him, especially now that we were surrounded by skaters more at his level.

There was nothing I could do but give him whatever time and space he needed, though. And make sure my skills reflected the time I'd spent on the ice rather than my competitive experience.

I whirled through the spin we'd been working on a few more times, counting out the beats in my head, picturing my partner whipping around next to me. Another skater cruised by, but my focus didn't waver.

Niko had booked us some private rink time, but we often took part in the freestyle sessions as well. By now, I was used to skating on the same rink as my competition. It hadn't taken much for my anxiety to dissolve.

No one was looking at us. They were all too busy worrying about their own routines to pay all that much attention to ours.

And when they were evaluating us, I thought we'd put on a pretty good show so far as our free skate program came together.

Seeing the time slot was just about up, I pulled off my skates, gave the blades a quick wipe, and sat down on the bench to pull on my sneakers. My own muscles were twinging with exhaustion, but it was a welcome burn. The feeling of work well done. Of dreams I was chasing so much more closely than ever before.

I got up with a heft of my workout bag just as the

skaters taking the next time slot spilled into the stands. Right at the front of the pack was Quentin Wolfe.

And just my luck, the cocky jerk strode straight down the aisle toward me.

His eyebrows arched as he looked me over. He stopped in front of me and tsked his tongue.

"I almost didn't realize it was you, Mrs. St. Pierre. What's with the new look? Figured you needed to play up that pretty face as much as possible to distract everyone from your partner?"

I rolled my eyes at him. If he'd had any idea what my disguise was actually protecting me from, the pompous asshole would probably have wet his pants.

"Some of us know that our looks are part of our performance too. And my name is Lou, by the way."

"Lou," he said with a mocking drawl, eyeing me with his piercing baby blues. "And where's the great Saint Jasper? Did he run for the hills when he heard I was coming?"

I didn't bother to hold back my guffaw. "Some of us also aren't paying that much attention to when everyone else comes and goes. Neither of us had any idea you were in the next time slot. I guess I'm just slow."

I shot him a sickeningly sweet smile that I knew would look obviously fake.

Quentin snorted. "I doubt that. From what I've seen, he's the one who'll be holding you back. Don't know why you decided to put your money on a fading star like him."

"You obviously haven't been looking very hard if you think he's fading," I retorted. "And after what I've seen of *your* version of skating, I'd rather be on the ice with him any day."

Quentin flashed his teeth at me, but the expression had the quality of a restrained snarl. "Considering who you call talented, my feelings aren't exactly hurt. You'd think him wimping out last year would give you enough of a clue, but I guess you'll find out who's willing to put the real work in."

I gave him a pointed look. "Says the guy who's standing around heckling a girl he's not even competing with rather than getting on with practice."

Quentin let out a cool laugh, but his eyes gleamed with what looked almost like appreciation. I'd seen how Jasper acted with him—doing his best to stonewall and ignore the other guy.

Maybe he liked having me sass right back at him.

I grimaced inwardly at the thought of this prick liking anything about me, but at the same time I couldn't deny that my heart had kicked up a notch too.

His antagonistic intensity made for a good target to let out some of the tension churning inside me, that was all. And as volunteer punching bags went, he was pretty easy on the eyes. The sharp angles of his handsome face matched his penetrating gaze.

It really was a shame those striking looks had been wasted on such a trash bag of a human being.

"*I* can recognize talent," he said with a hint of a sneer. "But it's not like I can stop you from wasting yours."

I flipped my ponytail over my shoulder and batted my brightly shadowed eyes at him with a confident smirk. "Come up with whatever excuses you want to justify this growing obsession with me. I think you're just glad you don't have to go head-to-head with Jasper again."

The light in his eyes sparked brighter with what might have been a flare of heat too, but before Quentin could shoot off another caustic remark, his phone buzzed in his pocket.

Muttering a curse under his breath, he pulled out the device. When he glanced at the screen, his stance tensed. His jaw flexed as he tapped out a response with his thumb.

He'd just sent it off when the woman who'd glommed onto him before sashayed down the steps and draped her arm around his shoulders. "Why are you bothering with this dope, babe?" She pursed her hot pink lips and narrowed her eyes at me. "Your time's up, isn't it, newbie? Let the professionals get to work."

She thought she was being professional? Jasper and Niko would never in a million years have stooped as low as these two did.

I tilted my head to the side with another stiff smile. "Oh, I've been trying to leave, but your boyfriend here just couldn't bear to let me go."

Quentin's lips curled. "Won't be the first time I'm in your way. Better get used to it."

He grasped Jess's hand and tugged her toward the ice, clearing the aisle. Swallowing my last snappy retort, I turned my back on them and hustled up to the doors.

Neither of them deserved any more of my energy. They were only on our case because they knew how good Jasper and I were.

Quentin should be thanking his lucky stars he didn't have to face off against Jasper this year. And Jess—I might not be totally confident in my competitive abilities yet, but I was sure I could wipe the ice with that catty bitch.

I even had a rival now. I really had arrived.

I laughed softly to myself and quickly changed, eager to get home and relax with the men who actually mattered. Should I tell Jasper about how antsy *his* rival obviously was around his return? Or would it just make him irritable hearing about Quentin at all?

Better to wipe the jerk and his stunning asshole face right out of my mind.

When I stepped out of the arena, I drank in the cool outside air, not caring about the tang of car exhaust. Boston was a hell of a lot bigger than Hobb Creek, but I loved that I still got to walk home from the arena when I wanted to. The guys had done an amazing job picking out our apartment.

I strolled down the street through the thickening twilight, peeking through store windows and perking my ears at strains of music that filtered through doorways. We'd be here for at least another month, and I couldn't wait to check out the clubs and music venues this city had to offer.

As much as I'd enjoyed Hobb Creek's peacefulness, I had missed a proper nightlife.

The cool air wound around me, but my jacket kept me cozy and warm. Knowing Rafael would be following along at a discreet distance warmed me even more.

Blending in with the big city bustle, I was ten times as anonymous as I'd been in Hobb Creek too. Anonymous and safe.

My bodyguard had never been one to actually hit the

dance floor, even though he'd followed me into Austin's clubs often enough. Would I be able to convince the other men to take a different kind of spin with me?

Niko would probably jump at the chance to let out more of his buoyant energy. Jasper would grumble about the idea… but he might get into it if I could convince him to give the scene a shot. If he brought the same athletic grace to the club that he did to the rink, he'd have everyone watching in envy.

The daydream brought a real smile to my lips. Tonight might not be the best time to go for it since Jasper had been extra sore, but maybe this weekend we could take a little break and work our muscles in all kinds of other ways…

I rounded the corner to our apartment building, my eyes flicking up to instinctively look at the windows of our unit. My steps slowed.

The lights weren't on, but I hadn't caught up with Jasper yet either. I'd assumed he'd gone on ahead of me and would already be here.

Hopefully he wasn't waiting back at the arena someplace I'd missed him.

I hurried up the steps, wanting to check what was up before I sent any worried texts. When I burst into the third-floor hallway, my breath rushed out of me in relief.

Jasper was standing right there at the threshold of our apartment, the door open in front of him. For a second, I thought I'd caught him just as he was about to step inside.

But rather than walking on in, he glanced over at me. The sight of his sallow face made my heart lurch.

As I dashed over to see what was wrong, Rafael

thundered up the stairs and charged into the hall after me. He must have noticed my sudden urgency and been afraid something was wrong.

Well, that wasn't incorrect, even if I hadn't known exactly how wrong at the time.

"Lou," Jasper croaked, stumbling backward. My eyes trailed from his unnerved face to his trembling hands and through the doorway.

Something lay on the floor in the beam of light that spilled from the hallway. Something white and red and feathery.

I blinked a few times before my mind fully processed the shape.

It was a dead dove.

Its body had been placed carefully in the apartment's front hall, its wings spread wide in a pool of dark blood that stained the tips of its pale feathers. And a rose lay next to it… No, *through* it.

The thorny stem had been shoved straight through the bird's neck.

My stomach lurched. I backed up too, colliding with Rafael who'd come up behind me.

"Shit." I ran my hands through my hair, brushing my bangs away from my face. "Shit, shit, *shit*."

Rafael's voice came out in a growl. "Stay here. I need to make sure whoever left that isn't still in the apartment."

He strode into the apartment, radiating protective fury. If the intruder *had* stuck around, they'd regret it very soon.

As Rafael's feet creaked through the apartment, the facts of the situation sank in with icy clarity. By the time he'd returned to us with a grim shake of his head indicating the space was all clear, my stomach had balled into a twist of anxiety.

"He followed us all the way here," I said, hugging myself. "That fucking psycho figured out where we went —he found the exact apartment in all of Boston…"

"He isn't going to get away with this," Rafael insisted, but I could see the concern in his dark gaze too. He didn't like this development any more than I did.

Jasper sucked in a breath, bracing his hand against the wall to steady himself. "We'll figure this out, Lou. We'll find a way to make sure he doesn't come back."

I swallowed thickly, my arms tightening around my torso. "I don't know if getting rid of him would be enough to keep us safe."

My partner peered at me. "What do you mean?"

Rafael would have already figured it out, but I had to say it out loud for Jasper's benefit.

"The rose… My mother's name, as part of her empire, is the Deadly Rose. The only reason he'd have included that detail is if he knows who I am."

And if this unhinged lunatic knew I was my mother's daughter… how long would it be before he tipped *her* off about my new life, and everything I'd achieved came crashing down?

NINE

Luciana

BY THE TIME Niko arrived back home with a few bags full of groceries, most of our collective shock had faded into a foggy confusion and burning fury. Rafael had gone through the apartment several times, yanking open closet doors and checking underneath all of our beds, examining every fixture for recording bugs.

At the very least, the stalker wasn't in our home anymore. It was another question entirely whether or not he was still nearby, but the only clue he'd left us was the dove itself.

Rafael and I had cleaned up the mess, but the horror that crossed my coach's face when we filled him in was like he'd seen it himself. My stomach twisted, half expecting Niko to rush to his room and start packing his things.

I'd told him about the "gifts" my stalker had left me

before, but that'd been well after the fact. And we'd hoped we'd left the sicko behind.

But after I'd explained everything, Niko sank into one of the armchairs, the horrified expression giving way to something more pensive. The rest of us sat down around him. I folded my hands over my belly as if I could hold back the ache that'd formed in my stomach.

After a minute of silence, the normally cheerful man glanced up at me with a somber expression that only deepened the ache. "What do we do now? Should we leave the apartment?"

I grimaced. "It'd be hard to find another one on such short notice, especially furnished, and it's not like we have the funds to set us all up in a hotel for days on end. If this asshole tracked me down here, I'm not sure moving would do us any good anyway."

"We wouldn't even need to think about that if he hadn't gotten this far," Jasper grumbled, and shot a dark look Rafael's way. "Isn't keeping psychos away from Lou supposed to be *your* job as bodyguard?"

Rafael's eyes narrowed. "I took every possible step to keep our location under wraps. I'm not the weak link here."

Jasper's shoulders stiffened. "What's that supposed to mean? I didn't tip anyone off. I don't know anything about all the criminal stuff."

"Exactly," Rafael growled. "So you'd better shut up about it instead of mouthing off as if you're in any position to point fingers."

"When Lou's safety is on the line, I think I—"

"Guys!" I pushed to my feet to stand between them,

holding out my hands. "Arguing isn't going to get us anywhere. We need to work together if we're going to deal with this prick."

The aggression deflated from both of their stances, though Rafael's scowl lingered. I pressed onward before he could toss out any more cutting remarks.

"We need to figure out who the stalker is, exactly what he knows, and what he's planning on doing with that info. Apparently he's figured out my ties to the Deadly Rose, but if he'd informed my mom of my location, her people would already be here. So he's up to something else."

Jasper let out a ragged sigh. "Okay. Could we put up some kind of security cameras? If he comes back, catch him on video?"

Niko perked up. "There's a camera in the lobby."

Rafael shook his head. "I already checked the footage. There was a guy who came in during the right timeframe, who's probably the right one, but he obviously knew he was being recorded. He had a cap on so the brim would hide his face, baggy clothes so I couldn't even tell you what his build is like, nothing distinguishing."

"But if we had a camera right in the apartment, he wouldn't be expecting that," Jasper said.

"Technology isn't really my forte," Rafael admitted reluctantly. "I wouldn't know how to set up something that'd go unnoticed—especially since he's already cased the place. If we stick a stuffed animal or a lamp or something like the typical hidden cameras, he'll be suspicious."

I frowned. "Well, we can try. It's worth a shot. But if it doesn't catch anything visible that we can use to ID him, it doesn't help us much. We won't even know he's been in the apartment until afterward."

Niko snapped his fingers. "You know, my sister's good with technology like this. She helped out a friend of hers who had a persistent ex-boyfriend hanging around messing with her things. She might have some ideas."

I shot Rafael a glare at his automatic skeptical expression and nodded at Niko. "Sure. It can't hurt to check."

"We don't want people all around the world knowing our business," my bodyguard muttered as Niko pulled out his phone.

"I won't tell her why we're asking. Just a general hypothetical situation." Niko tapped on the screen. "Let's just hope she's not too annoyed at me for waking her up. It's only eight am in Japan, and she likes to sleep in."

His eyes brightened, and he spoke into the phone. "Ohayo, Emi! Warui warui."

He launched into more animated Japanese that the rest of us couldn't follow, gesturing with his free hand as if she'd see his body language as well. I could make out a female voice on the other end in his pauses, so faint I probably wouldn't have been able to decipher the words even if they'd been in English.

I got the sense that she was offering some suggestions when his tone turned a bit serious again. He asked a few questions, I suspected in clarification, and turned cheerier with what I could tell was an expression of gratitude.

"Fine, go back to sleep, lazy bones," he added in English in a teasing tone, and turned to the rest of us as he ended the call.

"Well?" Jasper said, on the edge of his seat.

Niko beamed at us. "She said we could set up a motion detector by the door. It can be programmed to send us all an alert on our phones if someone enters while it's active. Then we'll know as soon as an intruder arrives."

Rafael leaned forward, his expression becoming more intense. "And I can get back here and catch the motherfucker." His lips curled into a fierce smile.

Jasper cleared his throat. "Whoever's closest and available should head back. Even if it's Niko or me. We don't want to risk losing our chance to nab the jerk."

Rafael raised an eyebrow. "It should be the one who'd know how to take him down. Which would definitely be me."

"No, Jasper's right," Niko said. "If he or I are close and can get here faster, we're not going to ignore it and risk him getting away. I'm sure we can manage to tackle one man and keep him from leaving at least until you get here." He flexed his bicep with a grin. "We've got plenty of muscle too, you know."

"Yeah." Jasper smacked his fist into the opposite palm. "And I'd like to take a few shots at the asshole who's trying to terrorize Lou. He deserves that and more."

The vehemence in his voice and Niko's unshakable enthusiasm sent a rush of anxious affection through me. I hadn't expected my skater men to be so determined to protect me in *every* possible way.

But here they were, declaring their intention to do battle for me without hesitation. Even though they weren't remotely prepared.

"He'll probably be armed," I reminded them, sitting

back down next to Jasper and grabbing his hand with a tight squeeze. "I don't want either of you getting hurt."

Jasper shot me a steely look. "And we don't want this prick doing anything else to mess with you. We can handle it."

"We won't do anything more than we need to in order to make sure he doesn't get away before Rafael arrives," Niko assured me with total confidence.

I didn't know how to argue with that, even though every particle of my body screamed to keep them out of this part of my life completely.

But I'd drawn them into it. I'd told them who I was and all the baggage that came with my old existence.

And they'd stuck with me willingly.

What were the chances that they would be more available to get here than Rafael would anyway? He'd be on patrol or guard duty, and they'd usually be at the arena with me.

"Fine," I said, with a firm glance at Rafael. "Whoever can come, will. Including me. But don't be afraid to fight dirty if you need to. A good swing of a skate or a heavy duffel bag could do as much for you as a knife."

And maybe we should get the guys some knives too. And make sure they knew how to use them well.

The thought made my head start to ache too. I pressed the heels of my hands against my forehead.

"We'll get it all sorted out quickly," Niko said, tapping on his phone again. "Emi knew a brand she's used before —she texted me a link to it at an American store where we can get it quickly. I'll place the order right now. There, done."

Jasper scanned the living room warily, his fingers twining with mine protectively. I didn't think I could stand to see all of my men so unsettled on my behalf any longer.

I got to my feet, tugging him with me. "Then we have a plan. I think we could all use something else to think about after all this stressing out, don't you? Why don't we check out that Cuban restaurant down the street? Rafael, you said you wanted to try it."

My bodyguard considered me, but maybe he could recognize my inner turmoil. Or at least that there wasn't much else any of them could do to protect me in this exact moment.

"I did," he said. "That sounds perfect, if these two gringos are up for it."

Niko laughed as he stood. "I'm always interested in trying out a new cuisine, especially with expert guidance."

As we tramped out the door together, a little of the tension inside me unwound. But the ache of anxiety lingered in my gut.

My men were as determined to defend me as I was to protect them... but what if this trick wasn't enough to stop the psycho who had me in his sights?

TEN

Luciana

AS OUR SERVER took away two empty plates that had once held heaping piles of masitas de puerco and empanadas, Niko leaned back in his chair with one hand on his stomach. "Now that's some food. I've never had anything like it."

Rafael raised an eyebrow at him. "Not many Cubans in Japan, huh?"

"Nope. I should encourage some to join us! The ones who already want to open restaurants."

Jasper laughed and licked a fleck of sauce off his thumb in a gesture that got me heated up just to watch. "I'm sure they'll really appreciate your enthusiasm. Those were only the appetizers, you know."

Niko straightened back up. "Oh, I'm ready for more.

But maybe we could get another plate of those little pork things too?"

To my surprise, Rafael let out a chuckle. "I think I could manage to put away a few more. This place can't quite match my abuela's masitas de puerco, but they're pretty good."

A smile touched my lips as I watched the guys. Rafael hadn't really hung out with my skaters before, joining us briefly for meals in the apartment but otherwise keeping his distance. He'd still been his usual quietly stern self since we'd headed out to the restaurant, but the other men's enthusiasm for the food he loved had obviously warmed him up to them a bit.

"Well, now I feel a lot better about letting you do the ordering for all of us," Jasper said with a relaxed grin of his own and perked up at the arrival of our server. "And here come the main meals!"

Rafael nodded to my partner's heaping plate as the waitress set it down in front of him. "That ropa vieja should be full of flavor. If it doesn't kick you in the taste buds, I'll just have to make my own version for all of us one night."

Jasper dug his fork into the shredded steak and hummed happily as he chewed. My mouth watered as I took in the Cuban sandwich arriving in front of me.

When I raised it to my lips for a massive first bite, Rafael shook his head at me. "I can't believe you. Out of all the traditional things they have on this menu, you go for the sandwich."

"Hey, I like what I like." I shot him a teasing smile.

"You should be glad I didn't insist on us going out for Polish instead."

Niko peered at me with curiosity. "You don't like Cuban food, Lou?"

"Not everyone's into the food of their background," Jasper pointed out. "And Lou isn't even Cuban—your family was from Mexico, right?"

"Yeah, four generations ago—pretty distant." I waggled my sandwich. "And I don't dislike it. I just like other stuff more."

Niko had turned to Jasper. "You aren't one to talk. You weren't even born in Canada but you pour maple syrup all over everything."

Jasper mock-glowered back at him. "I'm not that far removed. My parents only immigrated to the States a couple of years before they had me. Anyway, maple syrup objectively makes everything better." He glanced down at his ropa vieja. "Well, maybe it wouldn't work on this."

"Lou's nanny when she was a little kid was Polish," Rafael put in with a fond glance my way. "Got her hooked on pierogies and cabbage rolls. It's a goddamned tragedy."

"They're, like, the most comforting foods ever," I protested. "And pyzy—oh, man, if you've never tried those…"

Rafael pointed his fork at me. "You're not allowed to drool over Polish food while you have a Cuban sandwich right there in your hands."

I shrugged innocently and took another big bite. The savory pork was an awfully good treat too, but I wasn't going to admit that to him while he was heckling me.

"It makes sense that everyone has their own tastes,"

Niko said, between bites of his braised short ribs. "But I wouldn't trust a fellow citizen who doesn't love Calpis."

Jasper rolled his eyes. "I'm pretty sure not everyone in Japan loves milky soda, Niko."

"Everyone with good taste does." Niko smirked at him. "And one day I'll convert you too."

Jasper let out another laugh, and his free hand brushed across Niko's thigh. The other man's gaze darted to the gesture, and a soft flush colored his cheeks that I didn't think had anything to do with the spice in his food. He scooted his chair a little closer so their knees rested against each other.

I couldn't restrain a grin as I watched. The romantic side to their relationship was so new and fresh—it warmed me up knowing that I'd helped them finally figure out what they both wanted.

Maybe after Jasper got a little more comfortable with the physical side he'd never really explored before, the three of us could have a lot of fun, all together. Not that I'd mention anything along those lines just yet. Knowing Jasper, too much of a nudge would send him running in the wrong direction.

I squirmed a little in my seat with the pang of desire set off by the images that'd formed in my head and shelved them for another day. Seeing the way their faces lit up when their eyes met and they exchanged smiles, I knew we'd get there.

Then Jasper turned to Rafael. "You've obviously known Lou for a long time. How did you get into the bodyguard business anyway? That doesn't sound like something you'd find a job posting for online."

Rafael snorted. "No, it's a pretty different side of job searching." He paused, looking down at his plate for a moment, with a hesitation I didn't totally understand.

Was he still uncomfortable about the fact that we were hooking up now after he'd known me as a kid?

I reached over and gave his hand a quick squeeze. "My mom's… operations were pretty prominent. Anyone in town who wanted to get into that kind of work would have known she was the person to impress."

Rafael's odd reaction appeared to have smoothed away with my interjection. He nodded. "It's not the kind of thing most kids dream about, but I ended up getting wrapped up in the life… I still wanted bigger things than the local gang I started out with, though. Working for the Cordovas offered more opportunities."

Niko cocked his head. "Even when you ended up mainly protecting one person."

"One very important person," Rafael said firmly. "And I did get to travel a lot with the family. It wasn't all kiddy stuff. Especially once this one got older and wilder." He narrowed his eyes at me.

"As you should very much appreciate," I retorted with a cheeky flash of my teeth, but the conversation had reminded me that I'd never gotten much of Rafael's history out of him before. I knew I'd asked him basic questions when I was younger, but from what I remembered, he'd always deflected them.

"Your parents weren't in the criminal life, were they?" I said. "You always wanted to keep them away from that stuff."

Rafael's expression darkened again. "They worry less

not knowing. I made the choices I made—my parents shouldn't carry any burden from them."

He shoveled another bite of his dinner into his mouth with a firmness that suggested the topic was closed. I eyed him for a moment, wondering at his sudden clamming up after he'd gotten more talkative earlier.

Was there something about his early career that he didn't want *me* knowing? Or could it be that he was afraid of how the other guys with their much less questionable pasts would see things?

This wasn't the time to push him about it. Maybe when we no longer had the looming threats of both my stalker and my mom, plus the impending competition, hanging over our heads.

The waitress returned a few minutes later and beamed at us. "Look at all these clean plates. That's the perfect compliment to the chef. Is anyone ready for dessert?"

Niko elbowed Jasper lightly. "This one is always game for something sweet."

"Hey!" Jasper protested before his mouth slanted into a self-deprecating smile. "Okay, he's right. Rafael, should we put our trust in you again?"

My bodyguard appeared to relax a little more as he rubbed his jaw. "I think I can be worthy of that faith."

We ended the night with a coffee and a sweet each. Jasper and I both spooned rice pudding into our mouths while Rafael and Niko both powered through miniature caramel flan.

The taste of cinnamon filled my nose as I relished every bite. I set the spoon down and was about to comment on how obscenely full I was when a phone alert pealed out from Niko's side of the table.

All of us stiffened, my heart skipping a beat. Niko yanked his phone out of his pocket. Then he glanced around at the rest of us with a rough chuckle.

"It's just a text—from Emi, complaining that she couldn't get back to sleep. We haven't even set up the motion detector yet."

A giggle tickled up my throat. No, we hadn't, but that was exactly what I'd been thinking of.

As the giggle tumbled out of me, the tension broke with the guys joining my laughter. Jasper rubbed his temple. "I can't believe I nearly jumped out of my skin over that."

"I guess we're all a little on edge," I said, still smiling, but inside my stomach had knotted.

Tonight had been a good distraction, but we were going to have to face the psycho harassing me sooner or later. I just hoped that finally confronting this prick would be the end of it. I'd never asked for any of this.

All I wanted was a normal life, and it seemed like the universe was determined to block me at every turn.

ELEVEN

Jasper

THERE WAS nothing like having the rink to ourselves after the shared time slots we'd had for some of our practices. Lou and I swept across the ice in sync, my legs pumping at exactly the same beat as hers.

I glanced at her to check that she was still ready to try the adjusted lift that Niko had suggested we switch to for our short routine, switching to a one-handed hold to make it more impressive. She smiled at me with a barely perceptible nod and reached out her hand.

I swept her up, pushing her slender form into the air as I whipped us around. Her body balanced in my hands, stretched out as if she were literally flying.

My arms tensed slightly as I let go with one hand to stretch it out into the air as well. But I managed to stop myself from stiffening up too much, and Lou stayed poised above me like she was never meant to be anywhere else.

I swung backwards as I lowered her, watching her skates touch down without a single wobble. She grinned at me, her eyes alight with the exhilaration that took her from pretty to absolutely fucking gorgeous. My heart skipped a beat as I grinned back.

We went through the rest of the routine just to feel how it all came together, my spirits buoyed by the initial victory. When we locked into our final pose and then glided over to the boards to meet Niko, he clapped his hands in approval.

"That looked fantastic," he crowed. "Here, take a look."

He held out his phone to show us the recording he'd taken. Watching Lou and me soar across the rink was almost as amazing as experiencing it.

"I need to keep my elbow a little higher there," I noted with a momentary frown.

"And I need to keep that foot totally pointed," Lou put in. "But it's so close to perfect! We should be able to have it down by competition time."

She prodded my bicep. "When are you going to have those costumes finished, partner? I want to see the full visual, and we've only got a week left."

I narrowed my eyes at her even as her enthusiasm had another smile tickling at my lips. "Hey, good sewing takes time, Punk. I'm just finishing up the details."

"Having seen the fabrics you picked out and your past designs, I know it's going to bring the whole routine together," Niko said with the unshakable confidence he so often managed to exude.

Sometimes it irritated me that I couldn't totally buy into his confidence. Now… I couldn't help thinking it might be warranted.

I'd found myself partnered with two skaters who understood what was important to me on the ice—and were doing everything they could to help me get there. It'd been a long time since I'd felt this at home at the rink.

This might be the best I'd *ever* felt about my skating aspirations.

The thought hit me with a rush of affection. I couldn't help teasing my hand along Lou's jaw.

"It'll be incredible, because I've got two incredible people helping me make it happen," I said, and tugged her into a kiss.

The arena's air might have been chilly, but Lou's lips seared against mine with blazing heat. Just like that, I wanted to meld her whole body against mine, to indulge in the other sort of partnership we'd proven to be awfully good at too.

But even with the rink to ourselves, the open air felt way too, well, open. I let my tongue flick over hers in a teasing promise of more fun to come later and drew back.

My eyes met Niko's, my other partner on—and possibly off—the ice, and the urge gripped me to yank him to me too. To show him I was embracing every part of our collaboration.

The same hesitation that had held me back from outright grinding against Lou gripped me again. What if someone walked in at the wrong moment?

Getting romantically involved with one's pairs partner wasn't that unusual. Openly hooking up with your coach —especially when you were both men? That would definitely raise a lot more eyebrows.

The twinkle in Niko's eyes suggested that he'd picked up on my desire. I almost overrode my hesitations—but was relieved that I hadn't when the door banged open at the top of the stands.

Quentin Wolfe's coolly arrogant voice traveled down the aisle. "What are you misfits still doing here? It's our time now."

Just our luck, we had to cross paths with this asshole even when we'd booked a private timeslot. I let out my breath in a huff, but Niko spoke first in his usual friendly way.

"Don't worry, we're just wrapping up. I assume having two skaters packing up in the stands won't interfere with your practice."

Quentin strode down the aisle, that girl Jess who was always hanging off him and two junior skaters his coach was working with trailing behind him. "I get that you'd want to spy on our brilliance, but you'd better get out of here fast."

I snorted at both the ideas of us wanting to spy and of him being brilliant, and Quentin fixed his piercing gaze directly on me. Because of course he did.

"I'm sorry I missed any of your practice," he said. "I bet it'd have been a laugh riot. I'll have to show up a little early next time for some entertainment before the professionals get to work."

"Fuck off, Wolfe," I muttered, unable to stop the remark from dropping from my mouth.

"Let's hope your skills are a *little* better than your insults, or I'm not sure I'll be able to enjoy our inevitable win."

He slid on his skates and stepped onto the ice without a backward glance. I wiped down my blades, fighting a grimace.

He just liked jerking my chain. I knew that. I shouldn't let it get to me.

As much as his comment about spying had rankled me, I couldn't help glancing over at him and his fellow skaters as I swung my duffel over my shoulder. We hadn't crossed paths with Quentin here in a while. I had no idea what he'd been working on.

It wasn't as if it mattered what we saw when we were competing in different—

Wait a second. What the fuck?

Quentin and Jess were gliding across the rink side by side, glancing at each other to get into sync. As I watched, they leapt up and whipped around in matching double Axels.

Their landings were slightly off, and their coach beckoned them over to give a few tips. My stomach sinking, I strode up to the boards.

"What the hell are you two doing?"

Quentin cut his gaze toward me. His tone went from cool to outright cold. "You didn't think I would let you weasel out of a proper competition that easily, did you, St. Pierre? It wasn't a problem to get me switched over from singles to pairs."

"But—you haven't even been training—"

He scoffed. "It isn't as if working with a partner is that hard."

"Especially when he's got one like me," Jess put in, slinging her arm around his waist and cozying up to him.

Quentin offered her a smile that wasn't much more than a smirk and leaned in to nip her earlobe. Her breathy giggle set my jaw on edge.

I couldn't tell if he even actually *liked* her. This was just one more way to piss us off.

"You're such a fucking idiot," I snapped. "You can't possibly be properly prepared to make this work. Why would you rearrange your plans for that?"

Quentin ignored me long enough to flick his tongue across Jess's jaw and squeeze her ass. She giggled again and nuzzled his neck as he returned his gaze to me.

"We actually tried out a little pairs skating this year already, just to see how it'd go. So it won't be too hard to pick up where we left off. You bowed out before I had the chance to beat you last year. I'm not letting you run away again. It's going to be *so* much more satisfying to crush you head-to-head."

Lou let out a guffaw behind me. "Somehow I think we'll be the ones getting all the satisfaction. Including the satisfaction of not having to listen to your crap any longer." She grabbed my hand. "Come on, Jasper. We've got more important things to focus on."

Fuming silently, I let her drag me away, my free hand balled into a fist. That fucking prick and his oversized ego…

"I'll meet you two out front," Niko said as we ducked into our respective locker rooms.

I peeled off my sweaty clothing and rushed through a hasty shower, but even the cool water I set it to didn't cool my temper. When I stalked out into the hall, my jaw was still clenched, my nerves jittering with annoyance.

How was I supposed to relax and enjoy the strides we'd been making when I knew I'd have to face that jerk's stupid mug throughout the competition? Fuck, was he going to keep up the whole pairs thing all the way to Finals?

If *we* even made it that far.

My teeth gritted harder. Why was I letting him get to me? I was letting him screw me up when I should have just ignored him.

But I couldn't quite will the anger away, and that only made me more pissed off.

Lou emerged a minute later, took one look at my face, and tsked at me. "You're still stewing."

"He just—he did this *on purpose* to try to mess with me."

She stepped closer, setting her hands against my chest and peering up at me through her eyelashes in a pose I had to admit was totally delectable and at least a little distracting. "So don't be messed with. We're better than those two—we have to be when we have months more practice at skating together."

She had a point. Even through my frustration, I could admit that.

"I just wish I didn't have to think about him at all," I grumbled.

"You don't." She cocked her head. "Why do you care what he does anyway? He's just one more skater we'll be up against, right? There are lots of others."

I exhaled in a rush. "I know. But none of the others are set on taking me down a peg like he is. He just—he gets under my skin. All that talk about how there's no way I could be good enough…"

I trailed off at the ache that came into my gut with the admission. A familiar ache, but not one that'd originated with Quentin.

Lou's expression softened. "What? Did something bad happen between you two, more than just heckling?"

"No," I said quickly. "He's never done anything but mouth off."

I hesitated, wanting to shove the other memories that'd risen up back into the recesses of my mind where I preferred they stayed. But the concern in Lou's eyes loosened my tongue a little more than usual.

I owed her some honesty, didn't I?

She stayed silent, giving me the space to decide how much I wanted to tell her. Affection overwhelmed the painful pang inside me.

If anyone could understand my situation, it was her, considering that what she'd been through with her mother had been even worse.

"My dad," I said finally. "Whenever Quentin lays into me, it reminds me of the kinds of things my dad would say. He hated that I wanted to pursue this as a career so much—it practically broke up my parents."

Lou winced in sympathy. "I'm sorry."

"We're past that now." I hung my head. "I've just

always had this doubt in the back of my head about whether it was really worth it. If I'm going to accomplish enough to justify the stress I put them through over my choices."

"Jasper."

Lou raised her hand to touch my cheek. When I met her gaze, her dark brown eyes shone perfectly clear.

"It's already been worth it. You inspired me—you must have inspired hundreds of other skaters, maybe thousands, with your past performances. And all the people who've been touched by seeing you skate… I know you've got tons of fans."

"People I let down by not showing up at all last year."

"You didn't owe them anything if you weren't in the right place to compete. And now you're back." She beamed up at me. "And we're going to be amazing."

More of the ache melted away, but the tension didn't disappear completely, even as she tugged me toward the entrance where Niko was waiting.

She hadn't been there for all the fights and the cold silences and the snapped remarks. She hadn't seen the one person who'd always been there to support me break down in tears because of where that had led.

Maybe I'd accomplished enough already, but I didn't feel like I had. And if I failed now, I'd let down not just myself and anyone out there who still believed in me, but the incredible woman beside me too.

TWELVE

Luciana

AS I HEFTED my equipment bag over my shoulder and stepped out into the fading late-afternoon sunlight, my stomach grumbled in anticipation of an extensive dinner that would make up for all the energy I'd burned on the ice. I'd hung back for an extra hour during one of the group practice times to work on some of my forms while Jasper and Niko headed out to search for a final embellishment Jasper wanted for our costumes.

He'd better show me what he'd come up with soon. I'd only caught glimpses and gotten a vague idea from the measurements he'd taken.

I set off toward the apartment, picturing the heaps of pierogies I could be shoveling down soon if I could convince the guys to go for Polish tonight. But I hadn't even reached the end of the block when a hand caught my shoulder.

I jumped half a foot in the air and spun around with my fists raised, only to see Rafael looking both tense and sheepish.

"Sorry," he said. "I thought you'd hear me coming."

I shook away my nerves and lowered my hands. "I was dreaming about dinner. What's going on?" The turmoil roiling in his burgundy eyes set my pulse thumping double speed.

His mouth pulled even tighter. "The motion detector went off."

My heart outright skipped a beat with a jolt of chilly exhilaration.

"Perfect. Let's go catch that fucker and put him in his place."

Rafael gave me one of his patented long-suffering-bodyguard frowns. "*I'm* going to put the prick in his place. But first I'm going to put *you* in a room at the nearest hotel. I don't want you anywhere near him or on the streets where he could find you."

My eyebrows shot up. "Are you kidding me, Rafael? This asshole has been harassing me, so I'm damn well going to be there to take him down. Don't start treating me like a kid again."

Rafael let out a huff of breath. "It's not about seeing you as a kid. I'm still going to do whatever I can to keep you safe."

"Only as much as I'm going to let you. We're together in this. Now come on. If we stand around arguing any longer, we could miss the guy!"

Rafael glowered at me, but I stared right back at him with my chin raised. He knew I had a point.

With a growl of frustration, he turned on his heel. "Fine. But I'm going in first."

"No arguments here. I can play backup this once as long as I'm still in play."

"This isn't a game, Lou."

I set off next to him, matching his swift stride even with my shorter legs. "I know. And it's time my stalker found that out too."

We hustled back to the apartment building at a measured jog, Rafael scanning the street ahead as we went. I peered around us too, but I had no idea what I should be looking for. It wasn't as if the psychopath was going to show up draped with his bloody idea of presents.

Just as the building's brick face came into view up ahead, an unnervingly familiar figure ducked out from the entrance. I didn't get a glimpse of the guy's face amid his clothes, but he had on a cap with the brim tipped low and a baggy coat with the collar turned up, just like Rafael had mentioned when describing the man he'd seen in the security footage two nights ago.

Rafael obviously made the same connection. He swore under his breath and paused while the figure veered in the opposite direction from us.

He motioned toward the building. "Stick your duffel in the lobby so you're more mobile and let's keep on this motherfucker's trail."

I darted inside, shoved my bag into a corner, and rushed out, falling into step beside Rafael when he immediately started walking. He moved slower this time so we'd keep a safe distance from our target.

"Too many bystanders to tackle him out in the open like this," he muttered to me. All kinds of regular pedestrians were strolling along the sidewalks around us through the waning evening light. "We wait until he goes off the beaten path, and then we strike."

I nodded silently, my lungs constricting in anticipation. The man who'd been messing with me for weeks was finally right in front of me. I longed to sprint right after him and slam my fist into the back of his head, knocking off that stupid cap, but then we'd look like the aggressors to everyone watching.

We needed a little privacy to do this right.

Instead, I studied everything I could see of the guy from where we were trailing half a block behind. The tan coat fell to his thighs, the rest of him covered by dark baggy jeans and large tan boots. Like Rafael had said before, it was impossible to get a good read on his body type with that outfit.

I flexed my fingers with their heavy rings. What kind of fighter would he be? Was he carrying any weapons?

Well, if need be, I'd start by kicking him in the balls. That worked with just about anyone.

We'd only followed him for a few blocks when he swerved abruptly to the doorway of a large chain clothing store. As soon as he'd disappeared inside, Rafael motioned to me.

"We can't grab him in there either, but we might be able to get a look at his face and ID him. And we don't want to lose track of him if he tries to slip out the back."

We loped the rest of the way to the store and stepped in after our target. For a second, my gaze skimming over the other customers, my nerves jittered with the thought that we'd lost him.

Then I spotted his blue cap at the far end of the first floor, beyond several clusters of clothing racks. I snatched Rafael's hand. "Let's go!"

"Better idea." Rafael steered me in a roundabout route that took the guy out of our line of sight for a few seconds.

My heart pounded faster. "But—"

"Here."

My bodyguard had drawn up next to a shelving unit that rose from floor to ceiling, a checkerboard of open squares. Over the top of a stack of folded jeans, I realized we had a perfect line of sight to my stalker.

But he couldn't see us watching him. As I stared, he turned toward the front of the store, clearly checking for someone.

For us. He'd realized we were following him, and this was some kind of gambit.

But none of that mattered when I was now getting my first clear look at his face.

Tufts of blond hair showed beneath the cap, topping a pasty face with a hooked nose and a speckling of acne scars. His jawline was still hidden by his coat collar, but I made out a brutal-looking slash of a mouth that set off alarm bells in my head.

This was my psycho stalker. And I had no idea *who* he was.

"I've never seen this asshole before in my life," I

whispered to Rafael, and then noticed my bodyguard's expression.

Rafael's gaze had hardened, his muscular shoulders tensed and his jaw taut. "Of all the bad fucking luck," he growled under his breath.

"What? You know him?"

Rafael didn't answer, only pushed forward. Was he going to confront the lunatic right here in the store after all?

But before he could corner the guy, the baggy-clothed figure strode straight past us like he'd just realized he was late for an important meeting. Rafael sucked his breath in with a hiss and marched after him, shooting a wary glance around the store in case anyone noticed our pursuit.

We burst past the doors only a few steps behind my stalker—just in time to see him jumping into the back of a car with a wave of his phone at the driver.

He must have called an Uber surreptitiously while he was in the store and waited until it arrived before he left. Fucking hell.

The car pulled into the street. There was nothing we could do but watch it go, unless we wanted to end up in a jail cell.

I gritted my teeth, resisting the urge to stomp my foot in annoyance, and spun toward Rafael. "Who the hell is he? How do you know him?"

Rafael sighed, his narrowed gaze still fixed on the back of the car as it cruised off down the road. He spun on his heel and motioned for me to walk with him.

"Let's get back to the apartment and see what he got up to there. I'll explain on the way."

I wrapped my arms around my chest as we set off. "I'm ready to hear it."

Rafael grimaced. "That prick's name is Martin Haggard. He ran with the gang in Austin for a few years back when you were a kid, but your mother got fed up with him pretty quick. He was too unhinged, too unpredictable—lashing out when it wasn't called for, making trouble in our own ranks. He crossed some line, and she told him to get his ass out of town. I heard he went north, but not specifically where."

My heart sank. "All the way to Canada, apparently."

"Seems like it. Maybe he ended up doing business with those amateur thugs near Hobb Creek and that's how he happened to see you." Rafael shook his head. "Maldita sea! The shittiest possible luck."

So, my stalker really was a literal psychopath. Wonderful.

I suppressed a shiver. "Why do you think he's harassing me? It doesn't seem like he's told my mom that he's seen me—she'd have tracked me down herself by now."

"No doubt. Who knows, with him? I always got the impression he didn't even care about the money—he just liked doing whatever he could to make people squirm… or scream. And I doubt he has fond feelings toward your family after your mother ran him off."

Fuck. And this freak had stumbled into my new life? Into Jasper and Niko's orbit?

It was even worse than I'd been afraid of.

"You don't need to worry," Rafael said firmly, as if reading my thoughts. "I'll track Haggard down, find out if he's mentioned anything about you to anyone else, and end this."

The cool certainty in his voice settled my nerves. Then he glanced down at me, and something shifted in his expression.

"Do you want to be a part of that? Of ending him? It'd be your right, after what he's put you through."

It probably didn't say anything good about me that a flutter of affection passed through my chest at the offer. Rafael was proving that he did recognize me as an equal force in our relationship—even the darker side of it.

I hesitated, turning the question over in my head as we reached the apartment building and clambered up the stairs. "I'm not sure. Scaring him off would have been one thing, but this… I don't know if I want to get my hands *that* dirty again."

Rafael clearly intended to kill the asshole. It sounded like doing so would benefit all society. And a part of me longed to at least watch the jerk suffer the way he'd tried to torment me.

But I'd hoped I could put the murderous side of my old existence behind me completely. I'd only killed a few people under my mother's orders, and each of those times had left me feeling sick both physically and emotionally.

"You don't have to do anything," Rafael said. "I can take care of it all on my own. I'm happy to. But I wanted to give you the option."

"Thank you." I exhaled in a rush. "Let me know when you figure out how to find him, and I'll make a final decision about how involved I want to get then."

It was clear as soon as Rafael unlocked the door that

Jasper and Niko weren't back yet. Small mercies. Although they'd have gotten an alert too, so we'd have to tell them something.

Rafael flicked on the light and took in the space. "Motion detector is where it should be. Looks like he didn't notice it."

I couldn't see anything out of place at first glance around the living room. No dead animals or obscure messages.

I eased over to my bedroom and braced myself as I shoved open the door. But my crumpled bedspread and my half-unpacked suitcase looked completely undisturbed.

A noise of consternation reached me from the opposite direction. I dashed over to find Rafael making a disgusted face as he fished something out of the refrigerator into a plastic bag.

"I'm taking care of *this*," he said over his shoulder.

I wrinkled my nose and held my hand out. "At least let me bring the bag to the trash chute."

He passed it over. By the time I returned from down the hall, he was almost finished scrubbing the shelf where Haggard had left his latest "gift."

I glanced back toward the apartment door, my stomach knotting. "I'm surprised Jasper and Niko haven't gotten back yet. You'd think they'd have headed over as soon as the alert went off. I didn't think they were going too far."

Rafael shrugged and gave the shelf a few more swipes along with a squirt of cleaning spray. "They probably realized we'd be closer since we were at the rink and finished up whatever they were doing first."

After seeing how determined my skater men were to defend me, I wasn't so sure they'd have taken the development that lightly. Swallowing thickly, I pulled out my phone to try texting them.

Before I'd done more than tap out a few letters, a key clicked in the lock.

I spun around just as Niko and Jasper stepped inside, their gazes searching mine but their mouths set in matching sheepish smiles—and a new face bobbing up to peek over their shoulders.

"Oh em gee!" the slim Japanese woman cried out with a clap of her hands, her voice holding the same light accent Niko's did. She pushed between the two men with a swish of her sleek black bob. "You must be Lou! I'm so excited to meet you."

The next thing I knew, she was throwing her arms around me. I hugged her back automatically gaping at Niko.

He let out a rough chuckle. "Ah, we were a little delayed because of a surprise visitor. Emi decided it'd be fun to drop in from Japan."

"It's going to be *so* much fun," his sister declared with unshakeable enthusiasm, pulling back to grin at me.

I plastered a smile on my own face, wishing I could mean it more. But any happiness I might have felt at meeting part of Niko's family was drowned out by the roar of uneasiness reverberating through my head.

Just seconds ago, Rafael had been cleaning animal gore out of the fridge. Just how much more were my two way-too-different worlds going to collide now—and who else might get caught in the crossfire?

THIRTEEN

Luciana

I LOOKED DOWN at my plate of spaghetti as the waitress set it in front of me and suppressed the flash of memory provoked by the bright red sauce. My stomach clenched, but I made myself pick up my fork.

Jasper gave me a glance with a flicker of concern as he leaned over his own plate, but I'd had a chance to talk to him and Niko briefly away from Emi before we'd headed over to her hotel to dine in the lobby-adjacent restaurant. Not wanting them to worry too much, I'd told them that Rafael and I had followed up on the motion detector's alert and IDed my stalker.

My partner was clearly still in protective mode, but he also knew how well I could take care of myself. Jasper dragged his gaze away and brandished his own fork.

"This looks great. I'm starving, and I've got a bunch

more work to finish tonight to get those costumes ready to go."

Emi clapped her hands together eagerly. "Niko said you make your own. I can't wait to see them!"

I couldn't suppress a genuine laugh. "Join the club. He's been keeping them secret even from me, and I've got to wear two of them."

Jasper aimed a teasing kick at me under the table. "Tomorrow we'll try them on. Promise."

"I'm sure they'll only make your performance more spectacular," Niko said with a grin.

"That's why I had to fly all the way out here," Emi declared. "It wouldn't be the same watching on TV. And it's been too long since I've been able to check up on my big brother."

Niko pressed his hand to his chest in mock-offense. "It's my job to check up on *you*."

She giggled. "Well, you can do that better when I'm in the same city as you. But it looks like your friends have been taking good care of you."

She beamed around the table at us, and I felt a little of my uneasiness subside. It was hard to worry too much about psycho stalkers with a presence as warm and upbeat as Emi right in front of me.

Obviously friendliness and good cheer ran in Niko's family. And her vibrant chatter helped drown out the questions that'd been whirling in my head since I'd seen my stalker's face.

I was glad she'd suggested we get out of the apartment to eat, though. We had no idea whether Haggard might come back there… especially now that he'd noticed Rafael and me tailing him.

Emi paused her eager remarks to dig into her seafood fettucine, only to start swooning a moment later. "So good! It's been too much time since I had authentic American food."

Niko clicked his tongue at her. "It's Italian, not American."

"Well, we're *in* America, so almost the same thing. They don't make it the same back home."

A strange twinge passed through my chest, watching them together. You couldn't miss how much they cared about each other.

I'd never had a relationship like that. No siblings, and even my interactions with my mother had been far from warm. She'd warned me not to get too close to anyone at school, and it wasn't like I could have felt comfortable inviting any classmates over to our house anyway.

It must be nice, having family you could joke around with and count on like that.

"I bet they cook it differently in Italy too," Rafael put in, but he softened the remark with a chuckle. "But I do like the American version."

Niko pointed his fork toward Rafael. "This one will introduce you to all the Latin cuisine you could fill your stomach with. Can't get much of that in any way back in Japan."

A hint of a smile, enough to make my own stomach flutter, crossed Rafael's lips. "Always happy to expand my culinary horizons."

I had to appreciate how gracious he was being about the sudden visitor when he must have been dying to get out there and track down Haggard. He hadn't totally forsaken his bodyguard role—I saw his gaze sweep the restaurant every couple of minutes, watching for threats.

No doubt as soon as we left Emi at the hotel, he'd be off tracing leads.

I still had to decide how involved I wanted to get in his investigation… and the consequences that would follow.

The thought made my gut knot all over again. I managed to force down about half of my pasta, but the heaping plate was too much for my scattered nerves.

During a lull in the conversation, I dabbed at my mouth with my napkin and nudged back my chair. "I'm going to hit the ladies' room real quick before dessert."

Emi popped up from her chair. "Oh, I should freshen up too. I think I saw the restrooms on the way in. Here, I'll show you the way!"

She walked ahead with buoyant steps and pushed into the polished restroom with her purse swinging from her elbow. I ducked into one of the stalls and emerged to find her touching up her glossy pink lipstick.

As I moved to wash my hands, Emi gave the stalls a quick scan. We were alone in the room.

She lowered her voice to a conspiratorial tone anyway. "I hope my idea about the… what do you call it in English? Motion tracker? That it helped with your security problem."

She'd spent five years of her childhood living in the US and attending an English school just like Niko had, but it wasn't surprising her vocabulary had some limitations.

I hesitated, not sure exactly how much she'd figured

out or what Niko had told her—on the phone or since she'd arrived. "Um…"

"It's crazy that fans get so obsessed," she went on. "He was telling me in the car that you've been coping really well, though, not letting it affect your focus."

Not too much. But I was grateful that Niko had been able to come up with a reasonable story on the fly that wasn't as unnerving as the real one.

"Yeah," I said. "The motion detector did help, actually. We know who's been coming around the apartment now, so we should be able to make sure he backs off."

"Oh, perfect. I'm so glad. It must be very stressful."

She aimed a softer smile at me, and I realized with a jolt that she really was concerned on my behalf. It seemed she shared not just Niko's upbeat attitude but his sense of compassion as well.

"It has been," I said. "But your brother—and the other guys—have been a lot of support."

"Hmm, yes." Emi's expression turned sly. "In all kinds of ways."

My face flushed. How much had she figured out about my relationship with the guys? "Well…"

She waved her hand as if dismissing my embarrassment. "They've obviously all fallen for you. And good for you juggling all of them and keeping them happy. Why wouldn't a woman want three men's attention if she can handle it?"

I coughed, still off-balance. "I guess that's one way of looking at it."

Emi shot me a sideways glance and patted my shoulder. "Every time I've talked to Niko since he started training you, he's been in a brighter mood. So it must be good for him too. I'm glad he has you, even if you're—how would you put it?—keeping him on his toes."

"Good," I said, grappling with my awkwardness. "It's important to me that he's happy. That we're all happy. I've tried to be upfront with all of them, because it has gotten kind of complicated. I just… like all of them too much to want to pick just one."

"And why should you if they're happy? I'm impressed." She flashed me another grin and tucked her lipstick into her purse. "We haven't known each other for very long, but from what my brother has told me and what I've seen, you're a very interesting woman. It makes sense that they would all be interested. And I hope we can be friends."

Friends. The word shouldn't have made me balk like it did. But what the hell did I know about having a real friend, someone who wasn't paid to look out for me? Another woman I could gossip about relationships and all that other stuff with?

On the other hand, if having a BFF was like this, chatting away with smiles and encouragement, why wouldn't I want *that*?

"I hope so too," I said honestly. It might take me a while to get used to the idea, but Emi seemed like she'd make a pretty awesome friend if I was going to have one.

I hesitated and added, "I'm really glad you decided to drop in and surprise us with this visit. It's been great to meet you."

Emi's eyes sparkled. "I'm glad too. I needed a break anyway, but always better to spend it with good company. Now let's go see about that dessert!"

She tugged my sleeve, and we ambled together back to the table, Emi exclaiming over the posh hotel décor the whole way. When we dropped into our seats, Niko raised an eyebrow at her.

"Don't worry," she told him cheekily. "I didn't tell her *too* many of your embarrassing secrets."

Niko snorted, and Jasper cocked his head. "When do I get to hear these secrets?"

Emi set her chin on her folded hands. "Maybe if you let me have a peek at those costumes…"

As we drifted back into light-hearted banter, a weight settled in my chest, dampening my temporary high spirits.

My new friend had no idea what she'd arrived in the middle of—and how could I explain the whole story to her?

I'd just have to make sure she never ended up in a dangerous position. Keep myself between her and any potential threat.

We shouldn't have her over at the apartment again. Stick to meeting out on the town and at the arena.

Unless my stalker had already found out about her and worked her into his plans.

My teeth gritted, and my fingers tightened around my fork.

Haggard had better not touch one hair on her head, or I'd lose any qualms I had about dealing out a brand of justice even my mother would be proud of.

FOURTEEN

Luciana

I GLIDED over to the boards with a relieved exhalation, reveling in the burn of well-worked muscles that was spreading through my body. My hands moved to smooth the ruffles of my training skirt automatically.

We weren't going to wear the gorgeous costumes Jasper had finally revealed to me until the actual competition, but we'd stuck to similar if much simpler outfits for our last few practices so we were used to the overall feel. The skating dress wasn't quite as comfortable as my usual leggings and thermal tees, but I was too excited about tomorrow's competition to care.

Especially when we'd whipped through our routine today several times without any slips.

I shot a grin at Jasper, who'd skated over to join me.

"That was a perfect way to end the last practice before the official competition."

He beamed back at me. "I don't think it could have gone better."

"You're going to knock it out of the park over the next couple of days," Niko informed us, his eyes sparkling, and checked his watch. "You don't need me for the packing up part. I've got to go meet that representative from the winter clothing chain that's thinking of coming on as an additional sponsor."

"Give them a good pitch!" I said with an encouraging wave.

As we sat down on the benches to chuck off and wipe down our skates, a trickle of figures passed through the doors, ready for the next time slot, which appeared to be a larger group one. I tensed briefly in anticipation of Quentin's snark, but it appeared he hadn't managed to bookend our practice time today.

Instead, all of the kids hustling ahead of their two coaches were junior competitors in their early to mid-teens. A few of them shot us glances as they sat on other benches to lace up, but one kid who looked to be about thirteen paused and stared at Jasper, his eyes wide in his dark face.

I tapped my partner with my elbow, and he looked up. When he met the boy's intent eyes, his expression turned just as awkward. "Oh. Hi."

"I'm sorry," the kid said in a rush, swiping his hand back over his hair, which was twisted into short dreadlocks over a neat fade. "I just—it's so cool seeing you, Jas—I mean, Mr. St. Pierre. I've been watching you since you were in Juniors. Got a bunch of your performances recorded to study them and everything."

I'd swear Jasper's cheeks pinked a little. "That's—that's very flattering." He straightened up, gathering confidence in the face of the younger skater's admiration. "It's totally fine for you to call me Jasper. We're all colleagues here."

The kid hunched his shoulders as if in embarrassment. "I don't know if I'll ever get to the same level as you. I try."

Jasper hesitated and then pushed to his feet. "I bet you can. How would you like it if I gave you a few pointers? I don't need to rush right out."

The boy's mouth dropped open. "For real? That would be amazing!"

Jasper glanced back at me in question. I shot him a smile and a thumbs up. I couldn't think of any better way for him to end the day before the competition started than by basking in awed respect of a fan and up-and-comer.

"I'll see you later," I told him. "Have fun!"

Watching my partner step onto the ice with the younger guy set off a flutter of warmth through my chest. Jasper could still be a grouch, but getting back into the competitive circuit was helping him get his own bearings again. And when he wasn't all tangled up with insecurities, he was a sight to behold.

And not just for his looks, as incredible as they were too.

After a hasty change into street clothes, I headed out into the mid-afternoon sunlight with high spirits. My hand brushed my phone in my pocket, but the motion detector alert hadn't gone off since Haggard's intrusion the evening Emi had arrived.

He didn't seem inclined to take me on in public, and I'd have made him sorry for it if he had. Besides, Rafael would be trailing at a discreet but not immense distance behind me.

I was rarely completely alone.

I veered down a quiet side-street that offered a little peace on the walk to the apartment, daydreaming about how I'd spend the night before the competition. It was time to get out of my head and just relax. We'd done all the prep we could.

Maybe the four of us could meet up with Emi for dinner again. Then cuddle up on the couch with some popcorn and a movie, like a real date night. And afterward... who knew what we might get up to?

Just as my lips curled into a smile, engines roared down the street. I spun around to face two sleek black sedans that tore across the road and screeched to a halt by the curb right next to me.

Several burly men leapt out—and leapt *at* me. I dashed away, but another car pulled up just ahead with a few more thugs barging out in front of me.

Shit. I had no idea what this was about, but it obviously wasn't *good*.

Two of the closest men lunged at me as if figuring they'd grab my arms. In their dreams.

Thankfully, when I'd gotten changed I'd adorned my fingers with their usual chunky rings. Shrugging off my duffel bag so it thumped on the ground, I sent a fist slamming into one guy's nose. Another bashed the second guy's jaw, the metal edges scraping open his skin.

While the first prick stumbled, blood pouring down

his face, the other snarled and snatched at me again. I ducked and punched him right in the balls.

He staggered, but his companions were closing in on me in a tighter ring. I blew at my bangs with a huff of exasperation, glancing around at them.

"I guess you guys don't want to talk this out like gentlemen? Well, okay then. Your funeral."

A couple more loomed over me, and I lashed out with both my fists and my feet. My heel rammed into one guy's shin hard enough to provoke an audible crack of bone, and my rings slashed open another thug's brow deep enough to send a stream of blood into his eyes.

But there were still more of them, and they were backing me toward the wall of the nearest building. I couldn't let them get me pinned.

A few of them were pulling out guns, another a knife. I swallowed thickly. My rings wouldn't be much match for those.

My gaze darted around. There was an alley opening just ten feet away. If I could take off down there—

I didn't even need to complete that thought before a massive body charged into the midst of my attackers with a roar.

"Get the fuck away from her, you pieces of shit!"

Rafael's fists whirled through the air. He pummeled two of the thugs' heads together before they could even shift the aim of their guns and kneed another in the gut so hard the jerk spewed vomit as he crumpled.

Another asshole jabbed a blade at Rafael, and my bodyguard snatched his wrist. He snapped the bones like they were toothpicks. The idiot swayed backward with a howl.

Another goon raised his gun from a safer distance, his arm swerving between me and Rafael. "Not another fucking move."

"That's my line," Rafael growled, drawing his own pistol. "Try to take a shot, and it's a bullet in *your* skull."

The sound of languidly clapping hands broke the tension. Yet another man was emerging from the sedans, this one in a collared shirt and wool jacket that gave him a greater air of professionalism than his colleagues' jeans and hoodies. A shock of white hair sprouted up over piercing green eyes.

"Enough of that," the newcomer said in a gravelly, authoritative voice. "Everybody, knock it off for a minute or two."

His gaze flicked over the thugs and the two of us with an expression of bemusement, as if he wasn't sure whether to be annoyed or amused. A few lines veered from the corners of his eyes and mouth, but overall his face was smoother than I'd have expected given his stark white hair. Based on everything else, I'd guess he was in his forties.

The goons backed up a few steps, a couple of them limping, the one whose nose I'd broken still clutching it. One guy remained on the ground, groaning.

"Who the fuck are you?" Rafael demanded, his gun still raised.

The white-haired man didn't appear at all concerned about it. His eyes narrowed as he focused on us for a longer beat.

"Not someone you want to mess with. My name's

Sheeran, and I speak for the Harvester. I assume I don't have to tell the Deadly Rose's daughter who that is?"

A chill ran down my spine. The Harvester was another member of the Devil's Dozen, alongside my mother. One of the leaders of the thirteen biggest criminal syndicates that controlled all illegal activity around the globe.

He'd found me? How? Why?

"What do you want?" I asked, smoothing the nervous rasp from my voice as much as I could. I'd never actually met any of Mom's equals, but knowing how dangerous she was and how careful she was with the rest of them, they obviously weren't people you wanted to offend without knowing exactly what you were getting into.

The man smiled at me with all the warmth of a lion about to dig into an antelope. "My boss has heard that you've shown up in town to make claims on his territory on behalf of your mother. But you and she should both know that all of Boston belongs to the Harvester, and attempting to steal it out from under him is an act of war."

The bottom of my stomach dropped out, but I forced myself to simply scowl at him. "Where'd you get that load of bullshit from? I've got no interest in stealing your territory, and the Deadly Rose has no idea I'm even here."

Sheeran snorted disdainfully. "If you're going to lie, you could come up with a better story."

"She isn't lying," Rafael snapped. "It's the truth. It'd be a pretty shitty takeover, trying to orchestrate it with a single nineteen-year-old girl and one guy for backup, don't you think?"

My hackles rose at him calling me a girl, but I knew he

was only downplaying my strength to help us get out of this. Unfortunately, Sheeran didn't appear to be swayed.

"The two of you tore through half of the force I brought out here," he said. "That's not convincing me you're here to make friends."

I scoffed. "We're not looking to make friends *or* enemies. I didn't even know this was the Harvester's territory! If you come and attack me, obviously I'm going to fight back, but I came to the city to skate." I motioned to the duffel bag I'd dropped by the wall behind me.

"Skate?" Sheeran let out a guffaw.

"Yes," I insisted. "I've cut all ties with my mother. I'm not interested in her empire or your boss's. I'm a figure skater."

"Now that's the most ridiculous story I've ever heard." Sheeran's gaze turned into a full-out glare. "You can quit with the crazy lies. The Harvester wants you *gone*, ASAP. If you ignore the warning, there'll be consequences you won't want to deal with. Next time we won't go easy on you, no matter whose daughter you are."

Without waiting for my response, he beckoned his men toward the cars. "Let's get out of here, boys. Leave the little princess alone… for now."

"You've got it totally wrong!" I shouted after him as he slid back into the front passenger seat, but Sheeran ignored me. The thugs helped their injured comrades into the cars, and the sedans drove off down the street, leaving us standing there stunned.

Rafael quickly jammed his gun back into its concealed holster. "Mierda. That motherfucker… Come on, let's get back to the apartment before any other armed idiots come at us."

I set off next to him, my pulse thumping fast and my nerves jangling. "What the fuck was that? Who the hell would have told him I'm here to steal territory?"

"I have a pretty good idea," Rafael muttered. "Who's the only person we know of who has any idea who you are and that you're in town?"

My head jerked around so I could stare at him. "You think *Haggard* tipped off the Harvester?"

Rafael shrugged. "Who else could it be? It was bad enough luck that the one prick recognized you—it'd be insane if we'd somehow crossed paths with *two* of the Deadly Rose's former employees who had a bone to pick."

I rubbed my hand over my face. "This whole situation is fucked up. Now we've got the Harvester breathing down our necks because of that lunatic's stupid lies. And Sheeran wouldn't even listen to me!"

"Haggard does like tormenting you every way he can." Rafael grimaced. "If I can figure out where he's holing up in town… but that won't stop Sheeran from gunning for you."

I looked at the apartment building coming into view up ahead, but it didn't offer any comfort. Nowhere in the city felt safe now.

How was I going to compete tomorrow with this new threat hanging over me? With one of the Devil's Dozen expecting me to take off the second he'd snapped his fingers?

"I can't just run," I said even as the idea crossed my

mind. "I came all this way—I'm so close—and I'd totally let down Jasper and Niko."

"Your life is more important," Rafael said.

"Skating *is* my life." My hands clenched. "I can't let myself down either. We'll figure it out. We managed to deal with that gang back in Hobb Creek."

Rafael hummed in his deep baritone. "I don't know, Lou. These guys are a pretty big leap above those idiots."

I lifted my chin. "I know they are. But so are we."

FIFTEEN

Luciana

JASPER GRIPPED the top of the boards as we watched the pair before our free skate whirl across the ice. "Those two are pretty good. Costumes aren't as nice as ours, though."

He shot me a wry grin that made me laugh. It was easier to be relaxed after yesterday's short program performance, which we'd swept through to receive high marks. Going into the free skate, we were practically tied with two other pairs for the top spot.

Even the fact that one of those pairs was Quentin and Jess hadn't gotten Jasper down. Hell, if there was one area we should be able to beat the two of them without breaking a sweat, it was in the artistry I knew our routine exuded.

I ran my hand down the sea-green fabric of the skating

dress Jasper had custom made for this performance. It shimmered under the brilliance of the arena's fluorescent lights.

The rink where the qualifying competition was being held was even larger and grander than the one we'd been practicing in. Despite having spent yesterday here already, my breath still caught when I took the space in.

"They are pretty amazing," I said to Jasper, giving my hips a little shimmy so the short silky skirt rippled over them. "You captured the oceanic vibe that fits the flow of the music so well. We're going to look like mer-people soaring through waves."

Jasper outright beamed, a more open smile than I usually got from him. "That's exactly what I was going for." He looked me up and down, and his gaze turned sly. "And that color looks amazing on you."

I tapped him on the chest. "You look pretty damn stunning too, partner."

The color set off the gray-green in his eyes, and the fit showed off his brawny physique to impressive effect. He looked like the spitting image of Atlantean royalty, something melancholic yet hopeful all at the same time.

"I expect to hear at least one collective gasp while you're out there," Niko informed us, giving both of our shoulders a squeeze. "Probably two or three."

I glanced up to where his sister perched eagerly in the stands. "Or Emi will cheer loud enough to drown everyone else out anyway."

It'd taken her several minutes to calm down from her exclaiming over yesterday's performance. The memory brought another smile to my lips.

The pair before us struck their ending pose, and my pulse hiccupped. It was almost time.

But there was no room for insecurity. I was going to finish this, my first fully professional competition. The girl from Austin who'd been told over and over again that she wasn't good enough couldn't exist any longer. I had to leave her in the past and claim my future.

The judges conferred and passed over their score. Behind the glass of the press box, the announcer moved closer to his microphone. He announced the number—in the low nineties, good but not great—and then cleared his throat. "Our next pair will be Luna Garcia and Jasper St. Pierre."

I let out my nerves in one quavering breath and stepped onto the ice with Jasper. Niko gave us a confident smile and a thumbs up, assurance shining in his dark brown eyes.

Up in the stands, Emi whooped and cheered as we found our positions. I closed my eyes, imagining that I was here on the ice of our regular rink, that I was just about to skate for pleasure with my favorite people surrounding me.

When my eyes opened and found Jasper's steady gaze, I felt much better. All of Niko's confidence and Emi's enthusiasm found its way into my heart, and there was no doubt that my partner was just as dedicated to this moment as I was.

The music started. Jasper and I pushed off across the rink side by side with wide sweeps of our legs. From my peripheral vision, I caught the way my flowy sleeves billowed in the breeze my skating created—they fluttered and rippled with every lift and dip of my arms as if I were underwater, performing an aquatic dance for the visual pleasure of my viewers.

In this moment, I was a siren, a creature of music and art and desire. And I was going to make this audience fall in love with me—with both of us.

I knew I was succeeding the moment that we nailed our first lift. The applause rang out while I was still in the air. As Jasper carried me across the ice, my hands raised high and my head tilted back, I said a quick mental prayer. I could only hope the judges thought it as impressive as the audience did.

Four minutes of perfection, that was all we needed to make it into Finals. And from that point, there were only greater heights waiting for us to make it there.

We soared through our next sequence of jumps and spins without a hitch. I breathed through every motion, matching Jasper's rhythm.

My gaze slid across the audience, taking in their avid expressions in brief glances. Every pair of eyes wide with awe lifted my spirits even higher.

We swerved closer together in preparation for our next lift, and my gaze snagged on one particular audience member. A broad-shouldered man a few rows up, with a shock of hair so bright red it was really orange and a navy track jacket.

I only saw him for an instant before he blurred back into the crowd, but a chill washed over me. Hadn't one of the Harvester's men who'd confronted me and Rafael two days ago looked like that?

Had the Harvester sent his people to hassle me again since I hadn't left town?

My thoughts scattered. Jasper was here with me, and Niko, and Emi. I couldn't protect anyone from the ice, and Rafael might not see the threat in time.

If it even was a threat. I couldn't be sure that was the same guy in the fleeting glimpse I'd gotten.

In my distraction, I nearly missed my cue. I pushed toward Jasper a little harder than I should have needed to, and could tell from the second he hefted me into the air that my balance wasn't quite right.

Shit. My heart thudded against my ribs as I flexed my limbs, holding my position but also attempting to adjust my weight just a little.

It wasn't enough. My error threw off Jasper, but he managed to tense his arms before they wobbled too badly on the descend. Still, my blades hit the ice at not quite the right angle.

I stumbled, my fingers swiping just inches from the ice before I righted myself. Inches from a total fall.

A sense of sinking dread filled my stomach. I whipped around into the next sequence of the routine, but I'd lost the exhilaration that'd been buoying me up.

I launched into our synchronized triple Lutzes just a tad short on momentum and had to spiral out after just one and a half turns instead of the full two. Another jerky motion on the landing.

Shit, shit, shit. Everything was falling apart.

I focused on the music and the hiss of our blades over the ice, doing my best to tune out my worries. I'd probably just imagined the resemblance. I'd been on edge since the fight.

We could still pull this together. I couldn't let Jasper down.

We spun, crossed paths, and whirled around each other. Jasper gave my hand a quick squeeze before releasing it as if to reassure me he was still here with me, and affection flooded my chest.

It carried me through our triple Salchows—not as difficult a move as the Lutzes, but close enough to maybe make up for it. I still didn't feel the same grace and emotion I'd meant to convey with the whole routine, but at least we landed in perfect sync.

We had one more lift left too. At the swell of the melody, Jasper's hands found their way into mine, clasping my fingers firmly.

The moment that the violin began to trill, I pushed off and he whirled me high into the air. I let myself stretch out in his arms, one arm arcing over my head as if beckoning the judges and the audience to join us in the world we'd attempted to create for them.

I came back to earth in a rush, but only for a moment. The sequence ended with a series of jumps.

I pushed off, tossing myself into the air at the same moment as Jasper did. Twice around, down, and then flinging my body up again. For a few seconds, I flew like the angel Niko always said I was, spinning once, twice, the full three times.

If my foot didn't point quite as tightly as I'd like on the landing, I could forgive myself after that finale. I beamed at the crowd as Jasper and I raised our clasped hands up in our finishing pose.

Inside, my heart was still racing. Had I screwed up our chances?

Did we have bigger problems to worry about than our score—like a bunch of goons waiting to murder us all?

"Are you okay?" Jasper murmured to me under the applause as we skated to the stands. "It seemed like you got lost for a bit there."

I resisted the urge to hang my head while the audience was still looking on. "I'm sorry. I got distracted and didn't recover fast enough."

"You were amazing considering this is your first major competition." He slung his arm around my shoulders. "They were only minor slips. We should still do pretty well. Don't worry about it."

We both knew that he was just being nice, but I wasn't going to argue him out of his good mood. I swallowed down the lump of guilt that'd formed in my throat.

Beating myself up in front of him wouldn't change my performance. It'd just make both of us feel worse. As long as he was putting on a hopeful front, I could do the same for him.

Niko's bright smile shone at us from beyond the boards as if we'd been nothing but brilliant, and I could hear Emi letting out a few whoops as we reached the gap in the boards. But, just our luck, Quentin sauntered by right as we were easing off the ice.

"Is *that* what we were supposed to be worried about? All I saw was a couple of screw-ups and a lot of fumbling.

And here I thought you might at least *try* to give us a real challenge."

"Go fuck yourself, Wolfe," Jasper muttered under his breath, and tugged me over to Niko.

Our coach grabbed both of us in a hug. "You were fantastic. Don't let the little things get you down. The judges will see through them. No one else has given them anything like that final sequence."

I tried to absorb his confidence, but it couldn't completely ease the tension in my gut. I found myself scanning the stands for the man with the orange hair and navy jacket. If I could spot him and confirm whether it was or wasn't one of the Harvester's thugs.

But I couldn't make out the guy in the crowd. I wasn't even sure which part of the stands I'd seen him in.

And he could already be moving—toward me, or toward Emi if the Harvester's people had spotted her with me and the guys.

I barely heard the judges announce our score. Jasper let out a sigh that was mostly relief, but I thought it had a slight tinge of disappointment. "One hundred and two point four eight. That's not bad at all."

My head jerked around. "Didn't the pair that went on second get a hundred and five? They were within a point of us after the short program. We're already down to second place."

Niko rubbed my back. "It's fine. Still a very good showing for a qualifying round. And there are only a couple more pairs left to perform."

"How high do we need to be to qualify for Finals?" I asked with a sinking stomach.

Jasper shrugged. "It's all relative. Depends on the top scores from the other qualifying competitions. Usually second at any of them would be enough."

He kept his tone casual, but his earlier good mood had vanished, his gray-green eyes turned solemn. I sank down on the bench, my shoulders slumping.

Niko pulled out his phone. "From what I recall, none of the other competitions elsewhere have shown stunning results. Let me look them up so we'll have an idea where you rank overall."

The couple on the ice right now weren't particularly inspiring me with their pedestrian song choice or their sluggish movements, but it was hard to tell how much that was an objective evaluation and how much my own low spirits coloring my impressions.

I dragged in a breath and scanned the crowd again, keeping a particular eye around the section of the stands where Emi was leaning forward.

No one had moved toward her or us since we'd sat down. Everyone I looked at appeared to be focused on the skaters on the rink.

If the Harvester or his lackey Sheeran had wanted to make a point, wouldn't they have gotten on with it by now? Really, it'd have made more sense for them to come at me before I'd had the chance to skate so they could ruin my chances.

I couldn't totally regret my paranoia, though. Not when dismissing the flash of possible recognition could have cost me or one of my companions their life if things had gone in the opposite direction.

Jasper nudged me with his knee, and my haze of

thoughts evaporated. "Looks like there's only Quentin and what's-her-name left."

I made a face. "Not what I want to be looking at right now."

"Hey, we can heckle them quietly between the two of us. That could be fun."

I should have been relieved to hear Jasper talk about his rival so flippantly. But right then Quentin and Jess swaggered past us, Quentin shooting us a triumphant grin as if he'd already beat us and Jess pursing her lips in a mocking air kiss, and all I wanted to do was punch the both of them.

It was a hell of a lot easier to put on a good performance when you didn't have to worry about murderous criminals.

I'd have liked to surreptitiously mock them with Jasper, but the moment their music started up, my body tensed up.

They'd gone ambitious even though they'd come to the Pairs competition late. The accompaniment they'd chosen was much quicker and more intense than what Jasper and I had picked. But they must have believed they could match the pace.

I'd already known that Quentin could handle the technically difficult moves, but it seemed I'd underestimated Jess. My jaw went a little slack watching them whip across the ice.

It wasn't my preferred style of skating. Every movement was a bit stiff, a bit too calculated without the emotion and artistry that drew me in.

That didn't mean there was anything actually *wrong*

with it, though. Beat after beat, they sped through each move without a single fault. Their music blared through the speakers, the notes pouring forth at their quick-paced tempo.

They missed nothing—every waltz jump and side swipe of their skates was rendered in just the right angles. I waited for them to falter, for them to fail at something, *anything*, but every move and position was flawless.

They weren't pouring their heart into this routine. That much was obvious to me. The only emotion I saw on Quentin's face was the moment that his eyes met mine as he skated by and he flashed me a cocky smirk.

My hands clenched at my sides. The dick did know how to push people's buttons.

Even so, I couldn't deny that he was something to watch. With the fiery red costumes they'd chosen that highlighted his lean frame and muscular thighs, he kept drawing my gaze back to him whether I liked it or not.

The two of them ended their routine in an abstract pose that gained a massive outpouring of applause from the crowd. My heart sank. It was undeniable that the two of them were incredibly skilled. The audience knew it, the judges knew it, and unfortunately, so did Quentin and Jess.

Niko tutted under his breath. "Impressive talent, yes, but they didn't have an ounce of the passion you two did. Artistry counts with the judges too."

My heart kicked around in my chest like a bad motor as we waited for the judges' verdict. It didn't take them long to settle on a score. They handed it over to the announcer, whose voice boomed through the PA system.

"Quentin Wolfe and Jess Hendrix together have scored… One hundred and eleven point three seven points."

My hands dropped to my sides. They'd smashed us, a whole nine points ahead.

"We're in third," I said. The words came out flat. "I can't believe I fucked up this badly…"

Niko was quick to jump in. "Third is still going to get you into the Finals. I promise. This is the last of the qualifying competitions, and the average top scores are mostly in the ninety to a hundred and ten range. You're still going to be in the upper ranks overall, high enough."

"But at the bottom of the pack when it comes to Finals." I resisted the urge to hug myself, not wanting to show even that much weakness in front of my men.

I wanted to do better than scraping by. I wanted to earn the kind of cheers Emi had called out for us.

I wanted to rub Quentin Wolfe's face in our success. I wanted to make him and Jess eat their words.

Most of all, I wanted to show everyone who told me I couldn't that I *could*. Now Coach Balakin's admonishments were ringing in my head all over again.

No. This wasn't over, not by a long shot.

"We'll have a month to prepare," Niko went on. "And we know what we're up against now. The two of you will come back absolutely breathtaking."

Unless my nerves got the better of me again. Unless the other side of my life interfered at the worst possible time.

If I didn't get it together, I could ruin this chance for

both myself and for Jasper and Niko. They'd both worked so hard.

If I screwed up again, we were out for the rest of the circuit. Rank low at Finals, and Jasper and I could kiss any hope of competing in the US Championships or the international competitions afterward goodbye.

SIXTEEN

Luciana

EVEN THOUGH WE'D only come in third, the Okabe siblings were not going to hear talk of defeat. The sound of Emi's high-pitched praise filled every room of the apartment as she fawned over me and Jasper.

"Anyone with eyes could see your performance was so much better than that blond guy," she insisted around a huge bite of her meatball sub. We'd picked up dinner from a local sandwich shop to celebrate our qualifying for Finals —which did deserve celebrating, even if we'd only made it by a hair.

I couldn't help smiling, even though the mouthful of Philly-style cheesesteak stuck in my throat before continuing down. "Pretty sure the judges had eyes."

She let out a huff and patted my arm. "They got too caught up in the specifics of the moves. But you had all the passion! The little mistakes don't matter when you both showed how much the routine meant to the two of you." She aimed a smile Jasper's way too.

Niko came back to the table with a beer and gave me a quick hug from behind. "That's what I keep saying. Once you get your nerves totally under control, your combination of skill and emotion will be unbeatable."

I inhaled deeply, fighting with my guilt and my irritation over having lost to Quentin, of all people. I hadn't been able to tell the guys exactly what had messed up my nerves yet, since Emi had been with us since we'd left the arena.

From Rafael's knowing gaze as he watched the rest of us in his typical solemnly quiet state, he suspected the truth.

"I sure hope so," I said to Niko, and gulped down another bite of my sub.

He tapped his pocket. "I've already gotten requests for a couple of interviews, reporters wanting to cover Jasper's comeback. They'd love to talk to you too, of course, Angel."

My heart gave a little lurch, both excitement that we'd gotten that kind of attention and panic at the idea of having more of a spotlight on me. I was supposed to be laying as low as I could for as long as possible.

I couldn't comment on that in front of Emi, but the carefulness of Niko's tone told me that he'd already guessed I'd want to decline.

I shot him a thankful smile. "I think I'll let Jasper handle the reporters for now."

Jasper shook his head in mock consternation. "Abandoning me now?" he teased.

I wrinkled my nose at him. "Not on the ice."

Emi bounced in her seat with her irrepressible energy. "Oh, I wish I could stay to watch your skills grow. But I can only take off so much time from work before they get upset. Maybe I'll be able to fly back in November to see you at Finals, though."

My spirits lifted in a way I hadn't expected. "Really? It's a long way to home."

She waved off my comment. "If I can make it work with my boss, I'll be here. I haven't had an excuse to travel in a long time. And it'd be amazing to see you skate in person again."

I offered her a smile that was totally genuine. I could definitely get used to this whole friend thing. "I'd really like that."

"Good." She clapped her hands together and then yanked out her phone. "We need to exchange numbers. You can let me know everything that's happening for when my brother gets too busy to update me."

"I always reply to your texts," Niko said in mock-offense, and Emi's laugh pealed through the room.

I was sorry to see her go, but when she glanced at the time after polishing off her sub, her eyebrows shot up. "Oh, kuso. I'd better get a ride. I need to be at the airport fast or I'll miss my flight."

Jasper stirred, a look of concern coming over his face. "Do you need a ride? We've got a car."

Emi had already been tapping on her phone again.

"No, no. I've got a taxi coming now. You should stay and keep celebrating—you deserve it!"

She grabbed me in a quick hug and did the same with her brother. Niko picked up one of her suitcases to help her bring her luggage down to meet the cab. I found myself going to the window to give one last wave before she hopped into the car.

Rafael ambled up beside me. "You liked having her around."

My smile turned crooked. "There's something to be said for having a warm female presence in the room. Not something I have much experience with."

Jasper's brow furrowed as he joined us. "You didn't have many friends in Austin?"

I shook my head. "I didn't really have *any*. My mom didn't like me associating with people outside her circle, and most of the people working under her were men. And it's not like they were interested in making friends anyway, unless they were going to get something out of it." I rolled my eyes. "The few women who did work for Mom were always pretty standoffish, probably saw me as a risk. If they pissed me off, they'd have to deal with her."

Niko strode into the apartment a moment later, flicking back his smooth hair with its pink streak. "It is nice to have family around after so long. I'm glad you all got along with Emi."

"She's easy to get along with," I said, my full smile coming back. Then my stomach twisted. "But we need to do more than celebrate tonight. I've got to explain what happened that threw me off on the ice."

Jasper frowned and tucked his hand around my arm.

"You don't owe us a justification. Nerves can get the better of anyone. We all get it."

"But it wasn't just nerves." I bit my lip and moved to the sofa to sit down, to help steady me for the conversation. "You know Rafael and I told you that some men working for one of my mother's colleagues, part of that Devil's Dozen group, threatened me?"

The guys joined me in the living room, Niko's cheerful expression darkening. "Did they bother you again?"

"No. It might have all been in my head. But it's because of them." I sighed. "I thought I saw one of the guys who attacked me in the stands. Afterward, I wasn't so sure anymore. It doesn't really make sense that Sheeran would have looked for me there when he didn't even believe I was interested in figure skating. But in the moment, without being able to really think it through, I freaked out a little. I was worried he'd try to hurt one of you… or Emi."

Jasper's frown deepened. He twined his fingers with mine where he'd sat next to me on the sofa. "Do you think they'll really try something like that because you haven't left town like they asked?"

"I don't know. They might stick to only harassing me. But with this on top of Haggard's tricks…" I rubbed my forehead. "We need to deal with Sheeran too, get him off my back before I have to find out what he'd do next. And before he says anything to my mom about the war I'm supposedly starting."

Niko glanced at Rafael, who'd stayed behind the sofa at my shoulder. "Didn't you say you were going to look into this criminal guy? And Lou's stalker too?"

Rafael nodded. "I've been working all of the connections I have access to. I don't know a lot of people in Boston, but I managed to get in touch with a few old contacts. They haven't been much help in tracking down Haggard yet, but they confirmed that Sheeran is the top dog in the city on the criminal side of things."

"Makes sense," I said. "The Harvester would squash anyone who tried to go against his people on his territory."

"And Sheeran's boss must be awfully happy with him, because he's got a huge mansion in the suburbs and a collection of flashy cars, from what I hear."

I grimaced. "If he's doing well under the Harvester, he's got every incentive to keep the guy happy. Which includes kicking me out of town."

Jasper knit his brow. "I guess we can't fight back in a literal sense. He must have tons of people working for him."

"Yeah. And a show of overt aggression against Sheeran and his men would only make the situation worse. Like I really am trying to go to war with him." I rubbed my mouth uneasily. "Plus the Harvester would almost definitely bring it up with my mom then."

Rafael inclined his head in agreement, though he looked unhappy about it. "There's nothing good that could come of going head-to-head with them. Even if we had the full backing of the Deadly Rose's power behind us, which we don't, it'd be a mess."

Jasper gave my hand a squeeze. "Your mom obviously had to deal with guys like this a lot. What would *she* have done if she wanted to force someone to back off but couldn't be direct about it?"

I leaned back on the sofa as I considered the question. My mind drifted to the memory of Coach Balakin's bloody corpse, and I winced.

"Well, she tried to force me to back off from skating by killing my coach. Manipulating me into thinking our enemies had done it because of his connection to me so I'd be afraid to keep at it."

I sucked my lower lip under my teeth to worry at it, thinking through everything Balakin had told me over the years. "I bet that's also how she kept him under her thumb the whole time, forcing him to always tell me I wasn't good enough. He loved his kids and his grandkids so much. All she'd have needed to do was suggest that they'd meet some horrible end if he didn't follow her orders…"

Niko shuddered. "I can see why you'd rather stay away from her."

"Yeah," I muttered, but the wheels in my head had started spinning. "But that doesn't mean her strategies couldn't apply here. What if we could figure out something that matters a lot to Sheeran and his most important lackeys and show that we could destroy *that* if he doesn't leave me alone?"

Rafael's eyes darkened. "You want to start hurting their families?"

My stomach lurched. "No, no, nothing like that. Nothing *real*. We'd be bluffing. I don't want to actually destroy anything they care about. But Sheeran believes that I'm dangerous—that I'm my mother's daughter. So he'd think I mean business. We'd have leverage that could level the playing field."

Niko's eyes brightened. "That all adds up. Where would we start?"

I turned to Rafael. "We'll need to find out everything we can about Sheeran and his right-hand men—which means mostly *you'll* need to find it out, since you have the contacts."

"Hold on," Jasper said, and indicated Niko. "We aren't going to stay on the sidelines for this. I'm sure we can manage to scope out a couple of these guys if you need it."

My chest tightened at Niko's emphatic nod of agreement. "These are criminals. They won't be happy with you if they figure out you're watching them."

Jasper drew himself up straighter. "The same goes for Rafael, doesn't it? And they've already seen him with you —they know he's part of your mom's crew. You said that Sheeran didn't take your comments about skating seriously, so chances are good that he never bothered to look into it. There's a decent chance he has no clue who Niko and I are."

Even as my stomach knotted, I couldn't deny he had a point. When I looked at Rafael, my bodyguard offered a grim smile.

"You might have an advantage over me, just this once. I'll still do most of the digging, but your lack of connection to the criminal world could work in our favor once we know who we're checking up on. If you're sure you want to go in this deep."

"No question about it," Niko said without hesitation. "It's to keep Lou safe and make sure they don't stop her from skating—I'll do whatever it takes."

Jasper's expression had hardened. "Same."

For a second, unexpected tears pricked at the backs of my eyes. There was no denying their adamant devotion, even though I didn't feel as if I'd totally earned it after my screw-ups this afternoon.

But my men didn't see it that way. They were going to stick by me and support me no matter what.

I hated the thought of them putting themselves in danger, but how could I tell them no when I knew how far I'd be willing to go to help *them* if need be?

"We have to make sure you don't get into any situations that are too difficult," I said. "Nothing too far on the criminal side, just getting a sense of their everyday lives."

Niko took in my face and stepped closer to brush his fingers over my hair. "You know this world better than we do, Angel. We trust your judgment. But we aren't going to stand back while you and Rafael take on the problem by yourselves."

I raised my head. "All right then. Let's get started with Sheeran's closest associates—and we'll keep an eye out for the perfect opportunity to put the squeeze on the big dog himself."

And hopefully Haggard wouldn't throw any new wrenches into the works before we'd dealt with this one.

SEVENTEEN

Niko

AS I SIPPED my beer at the bar counter, the jumble of voices and raucous laughter around me had my nerves buzzing. I tugged at the hood of my new leather jacket, chosen specifically to help me blend into this crowd in a shadier neighborhood of Boston.

This was my third visit to The Hook and Tankard, a bar Rafael had determined was managed by one of Sheeran's main associates: Louis Elwort. The guy usually arrived in the mid-afternoon and left in the late evening.

If the skinny man with a receding hairline who looked more like a high school principal than a gangster could be a thug, then maybe my impersonating one wasn't such a stretch. I squared my shoulders, a little thrill passing through me at the sense that I was tapping into an inner tough side I hadn't been totally sure I had.

In any case, I'd managed to fit in with the regular clientele enough that no one had hassled me. My hood hid the telltale streak in my hair, although I doubted any of the patrons around me would have been familiar with my work on the ice.

They were all occupied with a different sort of skating: a hockey game broadcast on the widescreen TVs poised around the room. I studied the whirlwind of movement as the men around me let out a shout at a goal.

The hockey players surged across the ice, all sweat and muscular force. I'd bet they had the strength to pull off at least some of the moves I loved, but in their element, they showed none of the grace and precision I admired in a skater.

Imagining them spinning and leaping after the puck like one of my trainees made my lips twitch with amusement. No, they were simply doing what their job called for.

Still, there was something fascinating about the visceral aggression of the sport. Maybe sometime I could draw on it for inspiration for a particularly provocative routine.

At the edge of my vision, I noticed Elwort emerging from his office behind the bar. He'd left earlier than this the first night I'd come by but later the second night, so I couldn't read too much into his appearance.

Except that my instincts, honed by years of paying attention to the exact angles of a hand or a pointed toe, the tiny indications that a takeoff had come with enough momentum or a lift with the right height, caught a couple of telling gestures. Elwort tapped his hip pocket, where I'd determined he kept his keys. Then he shot a quick look in the mirror beneath the shelves of expensive liquor and flicked his fingers over his thinning hair.

He'd gone through those motions both times before, just as he was leaving. My pulse thumped faster.

I could take advantage of my observations. This time I might actually fulfill my mission here.

Leaving ahead of him would make me look much less suspicious. I drained the last of my beer and sauntered toward the doorway at what I felt was an appropriately macho gait.

The growl of Elwort's voice reached my ears as I passed him where he'd stepped close to the bartender. The chilling hostility in his tone dispelled the school-principal impression in an instant.

"If I catch you skimmin' tips, Larry, I'll have you more'n just fired. You won't be hard to replace."

The bell over the door jangled with my exit. In the cool evening air outside, I picked up my pace. The last two times, Elwort had headed east for a couple of blocks and then veered south.

The first time, I'd trailed a couple of blocks behind him all the way to a mundane apartment building that hadn't offered up any clues. The second time, he'd taken a turn and vanished from view by the time I'd reached the intersection.

I had to stay on his trail this time. Lou was counting on me.

And if I kept failing, Rafael was going to think he was right that Jasper and I couldn't hold our own when it came to protecting her.

Around the first bend, I ducked into an alley I'd noted before. The stink of the garbage cans farther down it had me wrinkling my nose, but the shadowed space made for an ideal hiding spot.

It was only a few minutes before the brisk thud of Elwort's footsteps approached. I pressed myself against the alley wall where the shadows were thickest and watched his slim form stride by.

After waiting for several seconds, I slipped out and started ambling down the street after him with an air I hoped looked reasonably casual. I kept my head low and my hands stuffed in my pockets as if I were lost in thought and paying no attention to anyone around me, least of all the man up ahead.

I'd never attempted anything like this before. My nerves jittered as I debated exactly how closely to follow the gangster.

Lou and Rafael had stressed how dangerous these people could be. I didn't think the knife Lou had ordered me to carry in my jacket pocket would do me all that much good if my target realized what I was up to.

But I was more than just her coach. I wanted to be a man she could turn to, a man she could count on for *everything* she needed. Lou deserved that from all of us, or how did I deserve to stand with her and call her mine?

I hadn't focused enough on other people's needs before, and that had led to the greatest mistake of my life.

Elwort glanced over his shoulder, and I pretended to be studying the windows of the buildings I was passing. Then he took an abrupt turn to the left that I hadn't expected.

Kuso!

I hesitated with my silent curse and then sped up to a jog so that I could reach the corner in time to be sure of seeing which way he'd gone next. When I peeked around it, I just caught the streetlamps' glow gleaming off his balding scalp as he veered down an alley.

It was as if he was worried about being followed and going out of his way to take a complicated route. My mouth went dry as I hurried after him, but the racing of my pulse came with a jolt of excitement as well as nerves.

If he was being careful, then that meant he was up to something important to him, didn't it? Exactly the kind of thing we wanted to discover.

I slowed before I reached the mouth of the alley and peered down it, the back of my neck prickling with the awareness of how easy I could be ambushed. But I made out Elwort's skinny form at the far end, swerving in a hasty right.

I loped after him, setting my feet as quietly as I could manage amid the bits of trash that lay on the uneven pavement. At the bend, I took a cautious glance around the worn brick wall.

It was a good thing I'd been cautious rather than hurrying right around it. Elwort had stopped at the far end of the alley where it met another street, his head turning as he scanned the sidewalk around him.

His shoulders hunched. I held myself perfectly still until he pushed himself forward, crossing the street.

Having seen his wariness, I let him get farther ahead before sauntering after him and stuck to the opposite side of the street. He was walking faster again, but he kept going straight for several blocks. Once, when he started to glance backward, I ducked behind a parked car before he could notice me.

Oh, Niko the spy was improving his skills for sure.

The shops we were passing, some closed for the night and others derelict, gave way to larger concrete warehouses. After we'd passed a few, Elwort stepped into a side entrance on the next looming building with a jangle of his keys.

I leapt behind a bus shelter poster just as he started to check his surroundings. There was a rasp and a click as he unlocked the door. When I peered around the shelter, he'd disappeared inside, the door swinging shut in his wake.

What the hell was he keeping inside there that he was so concerned about? Was it part of the gang's criminal activities, or something more personal?

I needed to find out.

Trying to sneak after him right inside the building didn't seem like a wise idea. Instead, I crept around the outer walls, peeking into each window I passed.

Around the back, I noticed a glow in one of the windows farther down. I stole over to it and found it mostly covered by a dingy curtain—but there was a gap that allowed me to see into the room.

Perfect. Between the narrow opening and the darkness cloaking me, it'd be nearly impossible for Elwort to notice me out here. The glass would be reflecting the light from inside.

I squinted into the starkly lit room, bracing myself for a scene of violence or drugged indulgence.

What I actually saw was… paintings.

Lots and lots of paintings.

Canvases stood against the walls in stacks, a few of them framed, but many not. A couple of them stood on easels—one a landscape lit with neon shades, another a portrait of a face with abstract styling.

As I watched, knitting my brow in confusion, Elwort walked into view with a palette. He dabbed his brush into a blob of paint and added a few small streaks to the landscape.

Wait. Had *he* painted all these pictures?

That possibility didn't fit with the principal image *or* the gangster image, which had already clashed in my head. Could these be part of his criminal activities after all? Forgeries he was passing off as originals?

None of the pictures I could see looked like any famous paintings or even styles I was familiar with, though. And the delicate care with which Elwort applied a few highlights to the sky of his landscape contrasted sharply with his harshly threatening words to his bartender.

What was this man up to?

He started talking, just loud enough that I could make out his crooning tone through the glass. "That's right. Just a little blaze of yellow here, and you'll be perfect."

Watching a man I knew to be a hardened killer cajole his artwork like it was a young child was one of the most bizarre sights of my life.

His head lifted. I understood why a moment later when a woman appeared in the doorway to the room, trim and professional-looking in low pumps and a dress suit.

Her hair was coiled in a loose bun, but her spiky bangs showed a little edge.

I hadn't caught her footsteps from my vantage point outside. Her voice reached me as clearly as Elwort's had, though. "Are you still working on that one? I thought you were finished the last time I came by."

Elwort sighed and lowered the palette. "Sometimes you need to let the image sit for a while before you can see everything it needs."

"Yeah, yeah." The woman crossed her arms over her chest. "Do you at least have the others ready for me to photograph? You promised at least five new ones. I have clients asking about your work, you know."

Elwort waved toward a stack of canvases to his left with a distracted air, his gaze still fixed on the landscape on the easel.

The woman looked as if she'd let out a sigh. "All right, I guess I'll set them up myself. It wouldn't kill you to get a proper studio instead of this godforsaken warehouse."

The man stiffened, his gaze jerking to her. "You know I have to keep a low profile."

"But you could be making so much more of yourself! If you'd let me set up a single gallery show, you could bring in a hundred thousand in one night, easy."

"I've told you before," Elwort growled. "It's not about the money. All this… it isn't something that goes well with my other line of work."

The woman shook her head. "Yes, yes, your mysterious day job. I'm just trying to do *my* job as your agent—as much as you let me act like one."

"If you don't want me as a client anymore, then drop

me. But as far as I'm concerned, what you manage to do is enough. The pictures get homes. I don't have to worry about my stash getting too big."

"Whatever you say, Louie."

The woman dragged a few of the pictures over to where the light hit them better and took out her phone to snap a few photos. I stared, absorbing the conversation I'd overheard.

These paintings really were Elwort's. Work he cared about enough to keep doing it in secret even though he obviously felt his regular colleagues wouldn't react well to the pastime.

I guess art isn't really encouraged in criminal circles.

That shouldn't have surprised me after what I'd heard from Lou about her mother's insistence on squashing her passion for skating. It wasn't as if I hadn't gotten plenty of attitude for simply being a *man* and going into a career many saw as emasculating, let alone a man who was meant to present an image of toughness and danger.

But if Elwort cared about his artwork so much he'd risk discovery to keep doing it… then I'd found exactly the point of leverage Lou and Rafael had been hoping for.

A spark of triumph lit in my chest. All the furtive stalking had been worthwhile. And now I could return home victorious and be done with cheap beer and hockey games.

I pulled back from the window and rushed away from the building as fast as I could go while staying quiet. I didn't slow down until I'd put a few blocks between me and Elwort's warehouse.

As I pulled out my phone to summon an Uber, my

high spirits wavered. The memory rose up of Elwort's eager intentness as he touched up his painting.

Were we really going to destroy *his* artistic passion?

Even knowing what he did with the rest of his life, my gut clenched at the thought. I set my jaw and shook off the momentary guilt.

Lou didn't want to actually destroy anything that mattered to these people, only to make them think she would. And she wouldn't have needed to go even that far if they hadn't attacked her in a far worse way already.

Whatever happened to Louis Elwort after I turned this information over was on him and his gangster colleagues, no one else.

EIGHTEEN

Luciana

I ONLY LET myself skate over to the boards when every inch of my body was aching and my breath coming in pants. Jasper trailed behind me.

"The adjustments are really looking nice." Niko offered us each a water bottle. "I think that with a little more work, the free skate will be even more stunning."

"It would have been absolutely stunning last time if I hadn't screwed us over," I grumbled. "I'll be more in the game next time, I swear. It's just —"

Jasper laid a hand on my shoulder. "You have a lot going on. We know. Don't worry about it, Punk."

I took a long sip of water, my body releasing its tension at his touch. They were both so confident in me, so sure of my abilities. If not for them, would I have ever realized the true depth of my abilities?

I wasn't sure, but I did know one thing: I would be forever grateful for their grand entrance into my life. The two of them had cemented themselves along with Rafael inside my heart for good. Those three men were all I needed.

Jasper chugged the rest of his water and crinkled the cheap plastic bottle. "We've got ten more minutes of ice time. You wanna squeeze in a little more practice or head out now?"

Niko cocked his head. "You two have been working really hard lately. Maybe loosening up on yourselves wouldn't be a bad thing."

Before I could answer, my ears picked up on a sound that now instinctively set me on edge—Quentin's laugh, ringing through the door at the top of the steps. Chock full of arrogance and spilling over with disdain. Something sharp twisted in my chest.

My jaw clenched. "Are you serious? What the hell is he doing here this early?"

Jasper sighed. "He probably found out we booked the time before his slot and figured he'd take the chance to mess with us. You know what he's like."

I grimaced. "Well, we can't stop even ten minutes early now. He'll say we're running away from him."

A second later, Quentin pushed past the door with Jess at his heels. Their coach and her other trainees were nowhere to be seen.

The two of them sauntered down the steps and lounged on a bench near the ice as if they were there only to watch. Which I guessed at this point they were.

Quentin's eyes glittered, hard with condescension and challenge. Jess simply wrinkled her nose at us.

I rolled my eyes as I turned back to Jasper. "No point in letting them see the little changes we've made. Let's go through the first lift a few more times."

He dragged his eyes away from the stands, his hands fisted at his sides. "Right."

"And here I thought you two were preparing to blow us away now that you've got a second chance," Quentin called. "Awfully boring performance so far. Oh, I'm sorry, am I distracting you?"

"Shut it, Wolfe," Jasper growled, his shoulders tensing more. He nodded to Niko to start the music.

As the opening notes pealed from the speakers, we glided through the first section of our routine. I tuned out all thought of the jackass watching us, focusing on the beats of the music and my connection with my partner.

But Quentin had always gotten to Jasper more than he did me. When Jasper raised me into the air, I could tell right away that his arms were a little too rigid. They wobbled slightly on my dismount, and my skate jittered against the ice before I fully caught my balance.

A snort followed us as we circled around to start over from the beginning. When I glanced at the stands, Quentin had slung his arm around Jess's shoulders, and she'd tossed her legs right over his lap. She nuzzled the side of his neck, and he tipped his head to the side encouragingly.

Excuse me while I barfed.

"I think I'm seeing your problem," Quentin said in a mockingly languid voice as Jess trailed her fingers down his chest. "No passion. Saint Jasper here doesn't know how to handle a woman—big surprise."

I had half a mind to stomp over there and see how well Quentin could "handle" me when I slammed my fist into his face. From Jasper's expression, he was gritting his teeth to hold back a hostile retort.

I set my hand on his bicep, ignoring the jerk. "Hey, don't worry about that prick. Nothing he says matters."

Jasper gave his broad frame a little shake. "I know," he muttered. But frustration still radiated off him.

If he tried again all wound up like that, he was bound to make a mistake, and then he'd only get even more upset.

My words weren't enough to distract my partner from his long-time rival, but as Quentin had just reminded us, that wasn't all I had to offer.

He wanted passion? I'd show him passion.

The idea set off a crackle of electricity down the center of me. I pushed myself forward, grabbing the front of Jasper's tee, and bobbed up on my skates.

Every thought featuring Quentin or Jess was erased from my mind as I curled my fingers into my partner's auburn hair, twisting the strands around my fingers.

"Lou —" Jasper started, but I cut him off with an eager kiss.

My mouth melded to his perfectly. His arm came around my waist, tugging me closer. At the flick of my tongue against his lips, he parted them so our breaths could mingle.

As I kissed him more deeply, reveling in the attraction and affection I felt with this grouchy but mesmerizing man, the stiffness released from his muscles. He stroked his fingers over my cheek and delved his tongue into my mouth in the start of a playful duel.

I gave his lower lip a graze of my teeth as I eased back, heat coursing through my veins. The same hunger shone back at me in Jasper's gray-green eyes.

His gaze didn't so much as twitch toward the stands. In that moment, he was all mine, his preoccupation with his rival wiped away.

I grinned up at him. "Feeling better now?"

Jasper smiled crookedly back at me. "Loads."

The silence emanating from the stands was telling. Neither of us gave Quentin and his partner a sideways glance.

Niko started up the music again, and the two of us soared across the ice. My heart lifted along with our movements. When Jasper hefted me up this time, I whirled through the air with him solid and steady beneath me.

The two of us felt like one person, connected where the palm of his hand met my center. I knew my expression was perfect, the angle of my arms spot-on, and his stance just as perfect. Pride rushed through my chest.

Jasper set me down at just the right speed and angle, and I glided a little ahead of him while grasping his hand. I knew I was beaming at him but didn't care.

"Once more?" I suggested.

"Sounds good to me."

We swept through the opening sequence with more confidence, and grace flowed through every movement. The exhilaration brought an awed giggle to my throat.

Jasper spun me around, poised in his arms—and my gaze caught on a reddish splotch on the door Quentin had stepped through several minutes ago.

Deep crimson red, like blood.

My heart lurched. Images flashed through my mind, each hitting me harder than the last.

Coach Balakin, his face sallow and twisted in pain.

The pool of scarlet staining his white polo shirt.

His body lying stiff and still.

An involuntary flinch ran through my body just as Jasper started to lower me. The jolt made me slip from his grasp. Before we could recover, I tumbled to the ice, landing hard on my thigh.

Pain bloomed through my leg. I was going to have a massive bruise there for sure. But I barely felt it over the blare of panic that'd set my heart thudding.

Jasper knelt next to me, his face taut with concern. Niko was hurrying across the ice to us too.

"Are you okay, Lou? What happened?" my partner asked.

My words came out in a breathless mumble. "The door—it looks like there's *blood* smeared on it. I—"

I clamped my mouth shut and shoved myself to my feet. Quentin shot out some stupid remark that I let fly right past my ears. All my attention was on the door.

I yanked on my skate guards in an instant and sprinted up the steps as fast as I could with my skates on. Jasper and Niko hurried behind me.

As we reached the door, Niko exhaled in a rush. "It's only paint."

This close, I could tell he was right. The splotch, about the size of a human head, looked as if it'd been smacked there by a swath of wet fabric with no clear texture. A few rivulets dribbled down from the main shape. The red was just a little too saturated, and a plasticky tang rose off it that was totally different from the meaty odor of actual gore.

The paint hadn't been there when Quentin and Jess had walked in. Someone had done this in the past few minutes. What the hell was going on?

I yanked open the door swiftly as if I might find the culprit standing on the other side.

Instead, I discovered that the paint didn't stop at the door. A longer smear ran along the wall in the hallway, fading out and then appearing again, all the way to the door to the women's locker room.

Just as I registered that, the locker room door burst open. A girl I recognized as one of Quentin's fellow trainees scrambled into the hallway with a shriek, her eyes wide with panic.

Shit. I hustled over to the locker room with the guys flanking me, wishing I'd had time to take off my skates. I shoved my head inside, called out, "Anyone in here?" and motioned for the men to follow me in when no one answered.

I took two confident steps before stopping dead in the center of the changing room. The streaky line of red paint continued all the way across the wall, cutting off at the widest, most blank part of the wall.

There, the smears thinned to form a picture—a sketchy body with its torn-off head lying across from a tattered neck. Crudely shaped letters arced across the wall above and below the gruesome drawing.

This will be you. That's what bitches get.

My stomach churned. I stared at the wall until the imagery was burned into my memory and then spun away, just as Rafael charged into the locker room after us.

He looked at the paint and then at me.

I held his gaze, holding back the urge to shiver. "It was Haggard. It has to be. He didn't figure he could get away with terrorizing me at the apartment anymore, so he's switched to the arena."

With every word, my shaky nerves hardened as anger flared inside me. How *dare* this fucking sicko bring his lunatic crusade all the way here, where he'd ended up terrifying girls who had nothing to do with me as well?

When was it going to end?

Rafael swore under his breath and gripped my shoulder with a reassuring squeeze that conveyed all of his own fury as well.

"That bastard keeps slipping through our fingers. When I finally catch him, I'm going to make him regret every fucking time."

"There's no way to set up a warning system here at the arena, is there?" I said. "It's not like motion detectors will do us any good when people are always coming and going."

Jasper frowned. "Do you figure he realized we had something monitoring the apartment, and that's why he hasn't been back?"

"Probably." Rafael let out a sound halfway between a huff and a growl and spun on his heel. "Grab what you need and let's get home, now. You can shower and whatever else there."

I didn't argue. There was nothing I wanted more than to get back to the apartment, slam the deadbolt into place, and curl up under a blanket with my men around me.

Of course, not even our current home was guaranteed to be safe.

We ducked back into the rink area to take off our skates and grab our equipment bags. Quentin and his fellow trainees were on the ice, except for the junior girl who'd dashed from the locker room. She was speaking to the coach while wringing her hands.

Good. Let Quentin's coach figure out how to deal with the mess. I had enough to navigate already.

The four of us hurried out of the arena into the dimming late afternoon light. For the first time, I wished we lived far enough away that we usually drove. I'd have felt more secure with steel walls around me.

But Rafael stuck close by my side as we walked, Jasper taking up the opposite position and Niko striding ahead of us with his gaze scanning the streets. Their determination to protect me hummed off them, wrapping me in a small measure of comfort.

As our building came into view up ahead, Rafael grunted and raised his chin just slightly toward a car parked on the other side of the street. "Looks like Sheeran's decided to keep a closer eye on you."

Tensing, I followed his gaze. The sedan was exactly like the ones that'd pulled up in the ambush last week.

A couple of men were sitting behind the windshield, watching us as they passed. They definitely looked like the type Sheeran had on his payroll. "You recognize them?"

"One of them, definitely. I've followed him a couple of times. Just act normal."

"No kidding."

I strode on as if I hadn't even noticed them, but inside, my emotions were roiling.

Why couldn't everyone just leave me the hell alone?

Niko glanced back at us. "The Harvester still thinks Lou is after his territory?"

I made a face. "Seems like it." I sighed and squared my shoulders. "But we've been building our leverage. Maybe it's time to start dealing with the people we *do* know how to tackle."

NINETEEN

Luciana

"YOU BETTER BEAT it if you know what's good for you, bitch!"

The man in front of me stared me down with an expression that wanted to be tough but just wasn't doing the job. No matter how firmly he set his jaw, I could see the fear in his eyes.

I had him by the balls—metaphorically, at least.

I cocked my head at a cheeky angle. "All I'm asking you to do is listen. You don't want to mess with me, I can promise you that. You definitely won't like me if you do." I craned my neck to look at the vintage car behind him. "And neither will your shiny little toy back there either."

The man let out a growl, his hands clenching, but he stayed where he was. I'd already told him that he and the rest of Sheeran's crew would be in *so* much trouble with the Deadly Rose if they kept harassing me.

The guy, Eddie Johnston, was another of Sheeran's top associates. It hadn't taken long to figure out what mattered the most to him: the gorgeous vehicle behind him, some foreign make that I didn't recognize but could tell was both classic and kept in tip-top shape.

I didn't really want to destroy a thing of beauty like that, but I'd reduce it to a pile of scrap if that was what it took to drive my message home and protect the people I cared about.

"I said get out of here," Johnston said in a not very convincing tone. "I don't want to have to hit a lady but —"

"But you will, is that right?" I gave him a mocking smile, hoping he saw the crazy in my eyes. "Don't make me laugh, asshole. Like I said, there's a very easy way out of this problem. I don't want any trouble. I'm not here in town to threaten your business. Convince your boss of that and leave me alone, and I'll happily steer clear of you too."

I raised a finger. "But if you mess with me, you can say adios to that sweet little ride. Hey, maybe Sheeran would let you borrow one of his. You think he likes you that much, Eddie?"

"Shut up," he mumbled. Any remaining fire was dwindling in his expression.

"I'd be ecstatic to stop talking and get out of your hair. I just want to make sure we understand each other. You're going to encourage your boss to stand down? It'll be even worse for all of you if the Deadly Rose finds out you came at me with no provocation."

Johnston bared his teeth at me. "I hear you, bitch. I got your message; I'll do what I need to. Just get the fuck outta here."

I slung my bag over my shoulder. "My pleasure. Hope I don't have to see you again, Eddie."

I strolled out of the garage feeling better than I had in ages. I wasn't going to let the Harvester's Boston crew push me around anymore; I wanted to do some pushing of my own.

Taking out some of my frustration on these pricks was more satisfying than I'd expected. They had it coming, and I had no qualms about making them squirm after the beatdown they'd tried to deliver the other day.

I slid into the driver's seat of my Grand Marquis, wiggling into the plush seat. "One stupid goon down. And one more to go."

The GPS directions told me that my second stop was in a residential neighborhood across town. I passed through a swanky area that housed some of the city's rich elite—Sheeran's kind of place—and into a stretch of slightly rundown rowhouses that must have still commanded a decent price because of their history.

The looming brownstones with their artful styling caught my eye even in the darkness. But there wasn't much room for admiration in my gut when I thought about the asshole I'd be dealing with here.

Robert Cullen was a major player. We'd dug up connections to three different women he'd been stringing along for years, each of them believing they were his one and only. The second had given him a son he doted on when he came around, but having a kid hadn't been enough to make him clean up his act.

He didn't clean up much in general, it turned out. I passed his address, circled around the block to park, and made my way to the backyard with a series of furtive dashes and scrambles, only to find the yard full of overgrown grass, rusty patio furniture, and scattered, mud-streaked toys from when he must have brought his son around.

I wrinkled my nose as I crept up to the back of the house. Rafael had texted me to confirm that Cullen had headed out for some nighttime business, leaving his house unguarded. Perfect for me to set up the element of surprise —and show that I had the skills to deliver on any threat I made.

Like many criminals, Cullen was overconfident. The lock on the back door was a little too complicated for my picks, but he'd left one of the first-floor windows a couple of inches open. Just enough room for me to pop out the screen and shove the pane upward.

I rolled inside and onto my feet with a soft thump. Looking around, my mouth pulled into a grimace.

The inside of the house was worse than the yard. I'd entered into the dining room—at least, I assumed that was what the room was supposed to be based on the large table in the middle, which was heaped with newspapers and takeout boxes. More lay strewn across the floor.

If he hated cleaning so much, the guy could have at least hired a maid service, for fuck's sake.

I crept over to the living room and found more food wrappers there, as well as several pieces of clothing tossed over the sofa. An unpleasant odor, a mix of food going bad and stale sweat, hung in the air.

Could this guy get more gross? How the hell had he managed to pull not just one but *three* devoted girlfriends?

Somehow I was guessing he never invited *them* over to visit.

Thankfully there was one armchair that held nothing except for an empty chip bag and a few crumbs. I swept them off and planted my butt there, poised in wait.

Every few minutes, I checked my phone. We had no idea when Robert would return, other than our past observations suggested he rarely stayed away all night.

I hoped he'd get his ass over here soon, because the smell was starting to make me queasy.

I distracted myself with a puzzle game until the rumble of a car engine sounded outside. I shoved my phone in my pocket and sat up straighter.

Cullen whistled a jaunty tune as he climbed the steps to the front door. He shoved it open, swaggered inside—and jerked to a halt when I switched on the lamp next to me.

I aimed a sharp little smile at him without getting up. "Welcome home, Robert. Nothing all that sweet about it, though." I kicked at the trash. "I'm thinking your three girlfriends wouldn't keep screwing you if they got a look at this place."

Cullen gaped at me for a few seconds before he snapped into overconfident prick mode.

"What the fuck are you doing here?" he demanded,

barging forward into the middle of the living room, ignoring the boxes crunching under his feet.

He didn't ask who I was, and the glimmer of apprehension mixed with the anger in his eyes suggested he already knew. He might have been present for Sheeran's attempted beatdown, or he'd heard about me from other discussions within the crew.

If he knew I was the Deadly Rose's daughter, then he should be well aware how deadly *I* could be… if I chose to live up to that name.

I folded my hands in my lap. "Relax, Robert. I'm only here to talk. I take it I don't have to introduce myself?"

More fury flashed across his face. "If you think you're going to weasel your way into our territory by—"

I held up my hand to stop him. "As I tried to tell Sheeran, I don't have any interest in your territory. I'm here on my own business that has nothing to do with your crew or claiming ground for my mother."

He scoffed. "Like we're stupid enough to fall for that."

I decided against telling him exactly how stupid I figured he was. "There's nothing to fall for. It's true. And you're going to go back to your boss and speak up in favor of staying *out* of my business."

"Why the fuck would I do that?" Cullen snarled.

I counted off the reasons on my fingers. "One, because it's true, and my mother isn't currently involved. But if you keep pushing, she will be, and I promise you that'll be awfully painful for everyone involved. Two, because I'm sure you have more important things to do with your time than spy on and harass me. And three, because if you *don't*, I know three lovely ladies I'll be having a chat with."

Cullen's eyes narrowed. "You can't even know—"

"What, about Bridget, Theresa, and Alison? I've got their numbers right here. I'm sure they'd be *very* interested in hearing about each other, don't you think so?"

For the first time since his initial shock, Cullen hesitated. A ruddy flush came over his face. "You wouldn't *dare*."

I shrugged. "I don't think I'm daring anything, Robbie. You're the one with something to lose. I know about Adam too. I wonder exactly how often Theresa would let you spend time with him if she knew you've been two—no, *three*—timing her since before he was even born."

Rafael had observed Cullen with his son, and so had one of his contacts. By all accounts, the jerk in front of me cared about the boy a hell of a lot more than he did any of his romantic conquests. He never missed a Sunday meet-up, went to the kid's school events and sports practices… The very picture of a devoted dad, if a fucked-up boyfriend.

We'd obviously planned our threat well. What I hadn't anticipated was just how upset Cullen would get about it.

"You fucking cunt!" He lunged forward, his face turning to purple, ready to snatch my wrists. Looking like he figured he'd snap my arms right out of their sockets.

I sprang to my feet, but I didn't even need to dodge. He hadn't made it past two steps before a deadly *click* sounded behind him.

Rafael stepped out of the shadows, his pistol aimed right at Cullen's head.

"I wouldn't," he snarled. "You listen to her, and your

life goes on like it always has. You take one more step forward and I'll make sure the last thing you see is your brains all over the wall."

Cullen froze, but a lingering tremor of rage ran through his body. "Fuck. Who the hell are you?"

"You don't need to know that. You only need to know that you're going to regret it if you lay one finger on this woman."

Cullen wasn't stupid enough to imagine Rafael's warning was a bluff. He held in place, practically vibrating with frustration.

I brushed my hands together and fixed him with one last glare. "You've heard my terms. Talk to your boss. Tell him you've seen enough to believe I'm not actually threatening your territory. One more attack on me and my friends, and I'll make sure you never see your son or your girlfriends again."

Cullen sneered at me, but he also dipped his head in a slight nod of acknowledgment. That was enough.

I stepped around him and brushed my fingers across Rafael's arm. "Let's get out of here. I think Robert's finally got his head out of his ass."

We walked out the front door and strode around the block toward my car. Rafael stayed silent until we'd climbed inside and I'd started the engine.

"Nice work, there."

"Yeah." I swallowed thickly, realizing a lump had risen in my throat as the adrenaline rush of the confrontation waned. A knot of doubt echoed it in my stomach.

Would Sheeran's men actually act on my demands in

the end? Or had I only succeeded in pissing them off more?

It'd felt good in the moment, but looking back, all I could remember was the fury that'd radiated off both men.

What did I really know about laying down the law? This was all part of my mom's legacy, the kind of life I'd meant to leave behind.

The life that kept nipping at my heels no matter what I did.

"Do you think this is actually going to work?" I couldn't help asking as I turned the car toward our apartment.

Rafael shot me a measured look. "I think it's a solid plan, better than anything I've been able to come up with. If I saw a better way, I'd let you know."

I blew out my breath in a huff, ruffling my bangs. "I just feel… weird. Most of the threats we've given I don't even *want* to act on. And this one… Cullen's girlfriends deserve to know he's been cheating on all of them, especially his baby momma. I just promised *not* to do that if he gets Sheeran to back off."

Rafael reached over and gave my shoulder a quick squeeze. "We all make deals we're not totally happy with to survive in this world, Lou. You've got her info. You can always find a way to tip her off after we're sure the Harvester doesn't have Sheeran gunning for you anymore."

"Yeah. I'll do that." If we ever got to that point.

But Rafael was right. When you were dealing with career criminals, there wasn't much you could do that would feel totally right.

This might not be how I wanted to live, but I had no idea how else I could defend the new life I was building for myself—or the lives of the men I'd inadvertently pulled into this mess.

TWENTY

Rafael

PATROLLING the neighborhood around the apartment always left me feeling a little more grounded than when I'd left it. Yeah, okay, maybe I was stalking the streets a little more often than was typical policy, but with all the stirring up of Sheeran's goons that we'd been doing, I wasn't leaving anything to chance.

If they tried to run Lou out of town again—or punish her for ignoring the Harvester's demand that she leave—I was going to be right here kicking their asses to kingdom come.

This afternoon, there was no sign of any trouble. Just regular people going about their regular lives with no clue about the darker underbelly their city held.

That was fine. They could keep their ignorance if I got to keep my peace.

As I rounded the corner to bring me back toward the apartment building, the phone in my back pocket buzzed. My hand leapt to it.

That was my newer burner—the one I'd been using only to reach out to my old contacts from my time working under the Deadly Rose. I'd wanted to keep the number those former acquaintances and colleagues got totally separate from everything else about my new situation.

You could never be too careful when it came to the Devil's Dozen.

This call could be more incoming information about the Harvester's Boston crew. Maybe even a warning about an impending attack—or the news that Sheeran had been ordered to move on to other things.

Hey, a guy could hope, even if I didn't put much stock in those hopes.

I hit the answer button and brought the phone to my ear. "Hey. What's up?"

The voice that carried from the other end didn't sound like any of the guys I'd been speaking to lately. "Rafael? That is you, right?"

My fingers tensed around the phone. I stopped in my tracks, every nerve going on the alert. "Who's *this*?"

"Hey, no need to pitch a fit." At the brief, hoarse cough of a longtime smoker, a picture started to form in my head—but it wasn't of anyone who should have had this number. "It's Gus. I'm sure you haven't forgotten me just yet."

Gus—Gustavo. One of my colleagues who'd worked out of Lou's family home. He'd generally been assigned to house guard duty, and I'd shot the shit with him maybe once a week, just to pass the time. We hadn't been close, but then, I hadn't gotten close to anyone in the Deadly Rose's outfit… other than Lou.

"How the hell did you get this number?" I demanded, alarm pealing through my veins even more sharply than before.

"No big deal. I heard from Manny that he'd talked to you and got him to cough up your number."

Next time I saw Manny, I was going to greet him with my fist. For fuck's sake.

"And?" I prompted in a voice stark with warning.

"And I just thought you ought to know what you left behind, you pendejo. Because it's a big fucking mess."

My teeth set on edge. "De qué hablas? Just get to the point, Gus, or I'm hanging up."

Gus sighed. "You took off with the daughter, right? Everyone knows you left town together. But Mireya is *pissed*. Like, I've never seen her like this before. She's crossing lines, launching beatdowns—she's a mad woman."

He was still talking in his typical don't-give-a-shit way, but a hint of a tremor crept into the last sentence. The Deadly Rose had gone so far she'd rattled even this asshole.

"I don't see what that has to do with me," I said tightly. "Luciana's a grown woman—she makes her own decisions. I didn't fucking kidnap her or anything."

"I don't think it matters, amigo. The boss is on a tear, like she needs the girl back *now*. I think there's some plan she was going to put in play that she needs Luciana there for, and she's raining down terror until she gets her way."

A chill coursed down my spine. "A plan for Lou? What kind of plan?"

"I don't fucking know. She doesn't fill me in on these kinds of things. But she's pulling out all the stops to find her, and when she does—it isn't going to be good for whoever she figures is even partly responsible."

"What exactly has she said about the thing she needs Lou for?" I asked, gripping the phone so tight the plastic casing started to crack.

There was a rustle as Gus must have shaken his head. "Nothing. She's just making it very fucking clear that we'd better cough up anything we know."

"So what are you calling me for, *amigo?*" I emphasized the last word with an edge of sarcasm. Gus definitely wasn't any friend of mine right now. "You figure you're going to trick me into giving up some intel that'll earn you a reward?"

"Fuck, no. And Manny didn't say anything about what he's talked to you about, so I haven't got a clue. I just wanted to tell you that if you know what's good for you, you'll make the girl come home or drag her back here yourself. There's going to be hell to pay for a lot more of us than just you the longer she's gone."

"Gus," I started, but there was a click and then dead air. The prick had hung up on me.

I glared at the phone, my lips curling into a silent snarl. Lou wasn't just *a* woman but her *own* woman, not her mother's tool. Who the hell was he to tell me to cart her home like she was a runaway kitten?

I debated smashing the phone but held on to it in the end. The burner couldn't be traced by its number, and if

Gus passed the info on to anyone else in the Deadly Rose's crew, I wanted to find out right away.

A cloud of uneasiness descended over me as I stalked the rest of the way to the apartment building. My heart got heavier with every step up to the apartment.

What was I going to tell Lou?

I walked into the apartment to find Lou at the kitchen table, halfway through the plate of leftover roast pork and rice I'd made us for dinner last night. She glanced up at me with the fork halfway to her mouth and a mildly guilty expression.

"I hope you weren't saving this for yourself. I just had a craving, and it *is* lunchtime…"

The sight of her devouring my cooking should have filled me with warmth—and other kinds of heat—but I was still too chilled by my conversation with Gus. I managed to give her a crooked smile and kept my tone even. "That's all right. I'm never going to argue about you appreciating my work in the kitchen."

She grinned at me, all boldness and cheek, and a surge of affection and protectiveness swept through me in a tidal wave. Whatever Mireya had up her sleeve for her, I wouldn't let it happen.

Lou raised an eyebrow, and I realized I'd been staring at her too long. "What's with the face?" she asked. "Something wrong?"

She was already dressed in her training clothes, ready to jet off to the arena as soon as she'd finished eating. Her face was painted with the garish makeup she used as a sort of disguise out in public. I could see her leg swinging even as she waited for my answer, probably counting the beats to one of her songs as she replayed the routine in her head for extra practice.

I couldn't tell her everything I'd found out. I couldn't put all of it on her shoulders when she had to focus on her dream. She was already dealing with too much—so much it'd nearly cost her the last competition.

It wasn't as if she could help me fend off the Deadly Rose's plans when I had no idea what those plans even were.

"Just got an unexpected phone call," I said casually. "One of my old acquaintances from the Austin crew."

Lou's stance tensed just slightly—so slightly I wasn't sure anyone other than me would have caught it. "What did he have to say?"

I shrugged. "Nothing we couldn't already have guessed. Your mom's on a rampage, pretty pissed off that you disappeared. So it's a good thing we've been laying as low as we have. And obviously the Harvester hasn't addressed your supposed invasion with her directly yet."

Lou hummed to herself. "So expected news and good news. You should be smiling about it—or have you kept that grim expression so long you forgot how?"

She aimed a teasing smile of her own at me to show she wasn't serious and dug back into her lunch. I propped myself in the doorway, watching her as my conflicting desires and responsibilities churned in my chest.

She would want me to tell her the rest of Gus's story. But there was barely anything else to it. If I jumped the gun on this situation, assumed it meant more than it did… I could cause just as big a catastrophe as I almost had years before.

No. I wasn't rushing in all hotheaded again. I'd get the full picture, and then we'd figure out what needed to be done.

Lou glanced up at me again, with a fond gleam in her dark eyes that nearly undid me. "You really don't have to worry. I know how to keep a low profile. I've begged off any interviews—and no one cares that much about this level of competition outside of the skating crowd anyway."

She was trying to reassure *me*.

"You've been doing good," I said, hearing my voice go a bit gruff. "I just—you know what your mother is like. She's only going to widen her search."

Lou's gaze twitched. I caught a flicker of worry crossing her face before she squared her shoulders and got up out of her chair.

"She can search away. She's not going to find me. Especially when I've got you by my side, right?"

She sauntered over to me, her brightly painted lips curving up like a scarlet crescent moon. Her hands walked up the length of my arms to wind together behind the base of my neck. I breathed in a lungful of her sweet scent.

When she stood up on her tiptoes to kiss me, I met her halfway.

I was the luckiest goddamn man alive to experience this heaven with a woman so precious. I closed my eyes, sealing the moment behind glass, this tiny scrap of peace inside our whirlwind of a life together.

I wouldn't let myself mess up this opportunity for her. She deserved more than what she'd gotten in life up until now, and I'd go through hell and back to see her finally have everything she was owed.

TWENTY-ONE

Luciana

I COULD ALWAYS TELL when Niko had something up his sleeve. The sparkle in his eyes gave it away every time. But today he was being unusually closed-lipped.

"Can't you at least tell us what you're thinking?" I begged for the thousandth time that day. We'd stayed all the way through the group practice period at the end of the arena's schedule, and the last of the other skaters were just disappearing through the doors. Any second, one of the staff was going to come and tell us that we needed to get going too. "It's not like anyone's left to hear."

Niko smiled mysteriously. "I wanted to be sure there was *no* chance of anyone seeing what we're doing. The arena manager agreed to leave the building open for an extra two hours tonight, and I can lock up. There won't even be a janitor around." He patted his hip to a jingle of keys.

Jasper raised his eyebrows. "What's the big secret?"

Niko glanced around the stands, and Rafael emerged from the shadows as if on cue. Had our coach even tipped off my bodyguard before telling us?

Rafael dipped his head to us with his usual stern expression. "I'll make sure no one comes back into the rink area from the locker rooms and then stand guard in the lobby once they've completely cleared out."

Curiosity itched at me as Rafael stepped out into the hall. "*What*, Niko?"

Niko rubbed his hands together, the gleam in his eyes only sparking brighter. "I was watching winning international routines from previous years, thinking I might get some inspiration. And I did. I want to change the second lift in your free skate to something even more challenging. We're going to add a throw at the end."

My heart skipped a beat. "A throw? It's already the trickiest lift in the routine." And it was the one I'd messed up in our qualifying competition.

But Niko was nodding avidly, bringing up a video on his phone. "That's exactly why it'll stand out—and impress the judges more than your competitors. This combination isn't seen very often because it's difficult, but I think you two are made for it. It works best when the woman is a lot smaller and lighter than the man, and most pairs are a little more evenly matched than you two."

Jasper and I gave each other an evaluating look. I couldn't deny that our size difference was particularly striking—that was something we'd played into more than once with our routines. Still, nerves gnawed at my stomach.

Niko held out his phone. I watched as a pair of skaters sped across the ice. The man—who was more than a foot taller than his partner and much broader—swept his petite partner up and over his head like it was nothing. She stretched out into a star position like our own while he gripped her with just one hand—and then in a near-blur of movement, she was spinning over his head again, descending to whirl across the ice in tandem, and immediately launching back into the air with a scoop of his arms to land a perfect triple Axel.

It was fluid and graceful and stunning—exactly the kind of vibe we'd been going for with the whole routine. I needed a moment to find my breath.

"It would be perfect."

Jasper nodded, his eyes alight now too. "I think we could pull it off with some practice. We have a few weeks left before Finals. Do you really think we can keep it a secret?"

Niko shrugged. "The longer we can, the less chance of anyone trying to top it. We'll only work on that aspect during our private ice time, and Rafael will keep a close guard. I wanted to be especially careful tonight when we try it out for the first time." He grinned at us. "If you're ready to try it out."

My pulse thumped quickly, but there was at least as much excitement as nerves in the swift beat. "Yeah. Let's do this! And smash the smirk right off Quentin's face."

Jasper laughed, the sound as sweet as maple syrup. "All right, Punk. We shouldn't rush it. Throws are where the most injuries happen. Even I know Quentin's not worth risking that."

I swatted him. "I just mean we should get started."

We watched the video a few more times and then a couple of other examples Niko had found. I studied every tiny movement from lift off to landing, watching exactly how the skaters adjusted their positioning and balance. Then we took to the ice ourselves.

"We'll start with a single rotation in the throw and work up to the triple," Niko said. "So you can get used to the overall feel of it before getting even more ambitious."

It quickly became clear that the skaters we'd been watching had made the move look easy when it was anything but. The transition from landing to Jasper propelling me back into the air left us wobbling, and once I slipped and bumped my knee, Jasper catching me just before I outright sprained it.

But we got up and went at it again and again. Sweat dampened my skin beneath my training clothes, but the assisted leap began to feel natural rather than awkward.

On my second complete single Axel, my blade hit the ice at a bad angle and I had to shove myself out of a fall with my hands. I brushed the frost from my gloves on my pants and straightened up with a surge of determination.

"Almost!"

Jasper smiled, his gray-green eyes fiery with matching resolve. "We'll get this. I'm ready when you are."

It must have been at least another half hour before we worked up to a double jump, but that change was easier than adapting to the initial throw. After a few shaky tries, I felt nothing but exhilaration as I whipped through the air.

When my skates touched down, one after the other, joy rushed through my chest.

This complex move would have stunned me watching it on television as a kid. Now I was actually performing it.

I raised my chin. "Let's go for the triple."

Jasper and I flew off into the lift one more time. The feel of his hands supporting me was nothing but familiar. My hair cascaded out in a crimson stream.

He shifted his arms, and I moved with them, tensing and flexing my muscles to match his movements. Then I soared out into the air, the momentum carrying me even higher and faster than before.

One—two—three!

I hit the ice already grinning. The impact radiated through my lowered leg, but I stuck the landing smoothly. I swung around in the finishing spin and then did a little happy dance on the ice with a whoop of victory.

Jasper was beaming too, his face flushed with exertion. Niko applauded avidly from his position by the boards.

"That was fantastic!" he crowed. "I knew you two could do it."

This would elevate our performance above all the others we'd seen in the qualifying round. It *had* to get us a top spot at Finals. And we'd already proven we were capable of nailing it.

The elation of that success coursed through my veins, and nothing could have felt more natural than grabbing Jasper by the front of his shirt and yanking him into a heated kiss.

As he kissed me back with total enthusiasm, an electric current zinged through my body. His hands were like lightning, the press of his mouth like rolling thunder. Our passion blended, mixing together to form an emotion so ravenous that I thought it would burst.

I wanted more than just a kiss—I wanted every part of him. And not just him.

I drew back from my skating partner to yank Niko over to us. An eager smile danced across his lips in the instant before they collided with my own.

His tongue delved in to tangle with mine while one hand trailed down my back to grip my ass. I arched into him, still clutching Jasper's shirt as well, my hungry growl reverberating between them. Jasper bent his head to kiss my shoulder.

The flashfire of our collision seared every other thought from my mind. We'd already been practicing far longer than a typical day—we'd accomplished more than we'd even imagined when we started.

There wasn't anything wrong with taking the opportunity to do a little celebrating as part of our cooldown, right? Rafael was standing guard in the lobby, making sure no one would interrupt our interlude.

We'd been so focused on training and dealing with my horrible problems lately that we hadn't taken any time to enjoy each other.

"Come here," I said in a demanding purr, dragging both men toward the stands. They came with an air of the same heady urgency that was racing through me.

We snatched up our equipment bags and hustled up the steps to the doors. In the hall, I shoved them toward the women's locker room, which would have emptied ages ago.

Pushing past the door, I tossed my bag aside, scanned the open space to confirm we were alone, and immediately tugged Jasper and Niko back to me.

Jasper's mouth collided with mine again, his breath scorching. Niko's deft fingers slipped beneath my shirt to stroke over the bare skin. The next thing I knew he was peeling both shirt and sports bra off me to drop them onto the floor.

"What a beautiful sight," he murmured before leaning in to suck the peak of one breast between his skillful lips.

I kissed Jasper hard, my whimper reverberating into his mouth, and raked my fingers into Niko's silky hair. My pussy clenched, and I could tell my panties were already soaked.

I wasn't quite far enough gone to forget about the sweat I'd worked up on the ice. There was a way to deal with that and make this encounter even more fun.

I hauled each of my men's shirts off in turn, drinking in their sculpted chests with appreciative eyes. Then I stepped toward the shower stalls and flicked one on with a swift motion.

As steam wafted into the air, the desire on Jasper's and Niko's faces flared hotter. Jasper reached for the waist of my leggings without missing a beat and dragged them to the floor, pressing a kiss to my hip as he went. "You're fucking spectacular, Lou."

I shivered with lust. "You're pretty amazing yourself. Both of you."

I made short work of Jasper's pants while Niko stripped off my panties. As I reached for Niko's pants, an even more delightful idea sparked in my head.

"Hey." I flicked my fingers toward Jasper. "Why don't you give me a hand?"

Jasper hesitated, his gaze jerking up to meet Niko's. His face flushed, but there was no mistaking the extra flare of hunger that lit in his eyes.

Niko smiled at him, sly but gentle. He reached out to Jasper, and the other man took his hand, awkward until the moment our coach eased him right over so their chests were almost touching.

With a sudden surge of boldness, Jasper touched Niko's jaw and brought their mouths together. A rough noise escaped his throat as they gave themselves over to the kiss.

Holy hell, that was one of the hottest things I'd ever seen. Two of the most attractive men I'd ever known locked together in their own passion. A different sort of joy glowed in my chest, knowing I'd helped them find their way back to each other and this shared desire.

Jasper's stance stayed a bit rigid, as if he wasn't totally sure what to do with the rest of his body. I stepped closer and stroked my hand across his back, dappling kisses along his arm and then Niko's. A little of that tension unwound.

Jasper turned back to me, cupping one of my breasts and branding the crook of my neck with his mouth. As I gasped, Niko joined in, claiming my lips.

Interlocked between the two of them, I couldn't suppress a pang of guilt that we were leaving Rafael out of the fun. But then, I wasn't sure he'd be up for sharing me in *quite* such an overt way just yet, when he'd only just gotten used to the idea of him and me hooking up at all.

We'd work up to that. Lord, imagine how amazing this would feel with all three of my men adoring me at once.

With a little help from Jasper, I finally got Niko's pants off. I pulled the two of them with me into the shower stall.

The water hissed down over us, the steam tingling over my skin. The stall was decently wide, but still a tight fit with the three of us. I couldn't say I minded being squeezed between my men's solid bodies, though.

They didn't appear to have any problems with it either. Niko leaned past me to capture Jasper's lips once more, and then they both focused their attention on me.

Jasper held me from behind, massaging my breasts with his thumbs swiveling over my hardened nipples, his tongue flicking over the shell of my ear to lap up a stream of water. "How do you like that, Punk?"

"Mmm, very good." My approval was punctuated by a gasp when Jasper positioned one of my breasts for Niko to devour it again.

As Niko offered up sweet torture with the flick of his tongue and the graze of his teeth, I squirmed between the two of them. My pussy was throbbing with need.

Jasper didn't leave me hanging. As my head tipped back against his shoulder, he dropped one hand to tuck in between my legs.

A full moan reverberated from my chest. I rocked with the rhythmic gestures of his fingers as they slid over my clit and the slickness of my opening.

"I think you could put that mouth to even better use, Okabe," he said in a low voice that practically made me come all by itself.

Niko released my breast to shoot a brilliant grin at

both of us and sank to his knees. He made his way toward his destination with teasing care, pressing his lips to my belly, my hip bones, and my thighs. Then Jasper made way for him, and Niko lapped his tongue right over my clit.

Between Jasper returning to fondling my tits, Niko eating out my pussy, and the hot water streaming down over all of us, bliss washed over me from every direction. I writhed between the two men, riding Niko's mouth and reveling in the bulge of Jasper's erection now pressing against my back.

I rubbed against him as I rocked with their attentions and then reached behind me to grip his shaft. As I pumped him up and down between my fingers, his breath spilled out across my neck with a ragged groan.

"Keep at it," he urged Niko. "Look at how she's loving it. I want to watch you make her come."

Oh, fuck. His heated words gave an extra jolt to the sensations building through my body. Pleasure spiked through me in giddy pulses with the movements of Niko's lips and tongue.

When I looked down, it was to see Niko caressing Jasper's thigh as he sucked on my clit even harder. The knowledge that he was getting us both off at once sent me right over the edge.

I bucked into his mouth, crying out and grinding against Jasper. Pleasure swept through my body, cresting higher with each stroke of their hands and mouths.

It wasn't enough. Even as the afterglow pulsed through my pussy, there was a void inside me that screamed to be filled.

As I recovered myself, I gripped Jasper's cock harder. "Fuck me."

He gave a rough, almost desperate laugh. "Hell, yes."

Niko had eased back with a satisfied smirk. I caught his gaze. "My purse—it's tucked in my equipment bag. There are condoms in it."

I didn't need to say anything more for him to dart across the room to retrieve a foil packet. As he dug one out, Jasper tipped me over on the tiled floor, my knees at the edge of the shower stall and my hands beyond it. He knelt behind me, the water drumming against his back and my ass.

Niko returned to us and passed Jasper the packet while stealing another kiss from the other man. I watched their mouths meld together with a growing ache between my thighs.

The second they drew apart, I pushed Niko down on the floor in front of me. "I'm not done with you yet either."

As foil ripped behind me, I bowed over Niko's sprawled form. His cock jutted from between his toned thighs, begging for attention.

I licked his length from base to weeping head, loving the hitch of his breath and the groan that spilled out after it. He tasted like salt and the sweetest of musks.

Niko stroked his fingers over my damp hair. "You have no idea what you do to me, Angel."

"Oh, I have a little," I murmured, and lapped my tongue right over the tip of his erection.

Then Jasper pushed into me from behind, filling my

pussy with the delicious burn he offered so well, and all I could do was gasp.

My head arced backward for a second, the pleasure of that first thrust echoing through my limbs. My eyelids had drooped with the sensation, but even so, I caught the slight movement of the locker room door across the room.

Was that just a draft, or something more?

I started to tense, peering over without being too obvious about it in case we'd need to take an intruder by surprise. Then I made out the face in the narrow gap where the door was standing slightly ajar.

I could only see a sliver of it, but that was Quentin's cool blue eye staring at us, the slant of his blond hair above it, his sharp-edged features clearly recognizable even like that. The light streaming from the florescent panels overhead caught on the ruddy flush that'd come over his face.

Somehow he'd managed to evade Rafael's initial sweep of the arena. He'd figured he'd spy on us, huh?

He was sure getting an eyeful now.

The tension in me gave way to a fresh wave of giddiness, turned even more delicious by a competitive zap of energy.

Quentin had taunted us about our passion. Let him be shocked by just how much we could bring to each other. It wasn't as if we were doing anything wrong.

Let's see how much cocky arrogance he could produce the next time he saw us. I'd laugh in his face if he tried to convince us he and Jess were so in sync by letting her paw him.

I lowered my head and sucked Niko's cock right into

my mouth. As I bobbed up and down over him, increasing the suction of my lips, Jasper eased in and out of me, matching my rhythm.

Niko's hips swayed to meet my mouth, his breath breaking into panting. When I swirled my tongue around his shaft, another groan thrummed out of him.

Jasper swore and thrust faster, deeper. I whimpered over Niko, letting the sound quiver through the movements of my lips and tongue.

"Keep going, Jasper," he whispered. "Fuck her just like that. Harder—she wants it."

He was right—I did want it. I rocked back and forth enthusiastically, willing Jasper to comply.

He didn't need more encouragement than that. To my delight, he pounded into me so forcefully stars started to sparkle behind my eyes.

My orgasm swelled inside me, overtaking me in a tsunami. I clamped my lips hard around Niko's cock, determined to take him with me. His tug on my hair sent me spiraling right over the edge.

My vision whited out with the final surge of ecstasy, the spurt of Niko's release in my mouth made it all the more satisfying. Jasper's thrusts turned almost frantic, chasing us to the tipping point, until he dug his fingers into my hips with the pulsing of his cock.

He bowed over me as he rasped for breath, his arm looping around my waist. As my own chest heaved, I spared a quick glance toward the door, but it had eased shut again. Our audience of one had vanished.

Let him stew on the spectacle we'd just given him. Ha.

Jasper eased me around so I was sitting between him

and Niko. Niko scooted closer, encompassing us both in a joint embrace and gifting us both with playful kisses.

"Well," Jasper said with a chuckle. "That was definitely something."

Niko nuzzled my cheek. "Our angel is awfully special." He leaned over to nip Jasper's earlobe. "Not to mention our grouch."

"Hey!" Jasper grumbled, but a hint of a blush touched his cheeks as if pleased by the teasing affection.

I grinned at both of them, full of happiness. We still had a whole lot of problems waiting for us beyond this room, but for a moment they felt awfully distant in comparison to the passion and tenderness we'd just shared.

TWENTY-TWO

Luciana

EVEN AFTER SEVERAL DAYS, the memory of the locker room interlude still gave me a tingle, both of remembered pleasure and triumph.

Shockingly, Quentin Wolfe hadn't intruded on any of our practices since getting a look at just how much passion me and my partner—and our coach—shared. Maybe because he'd realized how pathetic any of his snarky comments about our connection actually sounded.

Rafael glanced over at me where we were waiting by the corner of the Chinese restaurant for our takeout to arrive. "What do you have that little grin on your face for?" His flat monotone didn't quite hide his amusement.

I drummed my fingers against my thigh. "I was just thinking about Quentin. And how good it's going to feel to absolutely destroy him in two weeks. I don't know if I can wait that long."

Rafael snorted. "Well, you're going to have to. And don't get too cocky. You should focus on your own routines, and then you'll be fine."

I knew he was right, but still, it felt good to know we'd thrown our rival for a loop. I allowed myself one more smirk of satisfaction and then put Quentin out of my mind.

The heavy scent of garlic, soy sauce, and five spice powder filled the room, making my mouth water. I did enjoy it when Rafael insisted on cooking dinner, but there was something to be said for variety. And not having to do dishes.

My stomach grumbled. Rafael met my eyes, the mirth clear in his expression now. "A little hungry, are you?"

"You know it. I'm starving after the workout we had today."

Rafael opened his mouth to speak, a half-smile lighting up his face. Before he could get a word out though, he froze, his gaze jerking to the restaurant's front window. His brows slanted down in a mask of fury, his burgundy gaze suddenly burning.

My pulse stuttered. "What?"

"I think I saw Haggard passing by outside. He had his head down low, but I'd swear— Wait here. If it's him, I've got to run him down."

He dashed to the door without waiting for my response. The jingle of the overhead bell melded with the thumping of his feet, and then he was gone.

I took a step after him with an instinctive urge to join

the chase. The rustling of plastic bags being filled held me back.

Someone did need to stay for the food. And it wasn't as if Rafael couldn't handle one guy on his own. I didn't even know which direction he'd ended up heading in.

If he'd been sure it was my psycho stalker, I'd have followed him in an instant, no matter what he'd said. But maybe I should go along with his instructions just this once… to make up for all the times I undoubtedly wouldn't in the future when it mattered more.

When I turned back toward the counter, the older lady on the other side gave me a wary glance. Maybe wondering why my companion had taken off in such a furor. I offered her a smile I hoped was reassuring, and she dipped her head toward me.

"Just waiting on the pork belly," she said. "A few more minutes."

"That's fine." Hopefully Rafael would have finished his chase by then.

No, hopefully he'd actually caught Haggard and was ending that asshole's reign of terror right now by whatever means necessary. I still hadn't decided how much I wanted to be involved in delivering the well-deserved consequences, but if staying out of it right now meant I never had to worry about the psycho and his gory gifts again, I'd be okay with that.

My phone pinged in my hand. A text lit up the screen from Emi, packed with exclamation points and emojis in her usual way.

Hey! Can't wait for those Finals coming so soon! It looks

like I can't get the time off, so you HAVE to send me all the vids!!!

I grinned. Emi, like her brother, seemed to know just when I needed a smile, even from all the way across the world. I hit the reply button and started typing out a response, but before I could, another text buzzed my way.

Especially some videos of that new lift and throw combo you told me about!! It's going be STUNNING!!

I promise I'll send you a video of our next attempt, I wrote back. *It's coming along really well.*

I had to admit that talking with Niko's sister was like a breath of fresh air after the wary and distant interactions I'd had with the women in my past life. Since we'd left, I'd found myself swapping stories about our interests and pasts with her.

I just wished I didn't have to deal with the twinge of guilt about how much of my past I was hiding from her. But I never wanted to be dragged into that world again. If I didn't have to worry Emi with all that garbage, then I wouldn't. I wanted her to see me as a normal person, not a former criminal or a charity case.

The woman behind the counter hooked a finger at me and set two bags down on the surface between us. "Your food is ready, miss."

"Thank you!" I pocketed my phone and grabbed both bags, one in each hand. The heat and the delicious scents wafting off them made my stomach gurgle again.

I considered the closed door that Rafael hadn't yet returned through and decided to wait outside. Maybe I'd see him already on his way back and I could meet him halfway.

As I stepped onto the sidewalk, the chilly fall breeze wrapped around me. The restaurant stood on a quiet side-street, just a few buildings down from a busy thoroughfare but with only the occasional passing pedestrian and car right in front of it at this time in the late evening.

No sign of Rafael in either direction yet. Frowning, I ambled a little farther down the street and decided to text him to see if he was finished checking up on his suspicion. If he didn't answer, I'd head back to the apartment on my own. It was only a couple of blocks.

I didn't even have time to reach for my phone before several figures burst from an alley across the street, charging straight toward me.

Sheeran's goons, I thought in the split-second it took to register the attack, and then I was whipping into action.

The thugs swarmed around me, throwing punches and ramming knees from all sides. I spun around, making use of everything I had in reach.

One takeout bag bashed into a prick's face, spurting hot sauce into his eyes. The other thumped a second attacker in the gut. I kicked it to send spicy noodles straight into a third jerk's mug, mourning the loss of our tasty dinner.

The second my hands were free, I lashed out with my ringed fists as well. The metal ridges carved lines through a goon's cheek, and I clocked another in the nose hard enough that he reeled backward.

It wasn't enough. There were too many of them, and they weren't holding back to deliver a warning this time. They wanted a total beatdown.

I whipped this way and that, stomping and jabbing,

but there always seemed to be another fist to dodge. My breath turned ragged in my throat.

I fumbled in my pocket for the knife I kept on me, but the second I yanked it free, another thug caught my wrist. He twisted it so hard the bones creaked and the blade fell from my hand with a spasm of pain.

Shit, shit, shit.

"Get away, you fuckers!" I hollered. "Let me go!"

At this point, I'd welcome a police siren if it'd buy me an opening to flee. I knew when I was overpowered.

I managed to heel the guy who'd snatched my wrist in the shin and then kick him in the groin, but as he stumbled backward, two more goons leapt on me. One of them tackled me to the sidewalk, my skull glancing off the concrete. As my thoughts spun, they held me down.

"Sheeran sends his regards, Princess," one of them snarled. "You should have run when you had the chance."

I flailed with all my might, jerking my arms free, but it seemed like a dozen feet were slamming at my body now. Ducking my head, I raised my arms to shield it as best I could. More blows battered my chest and abdomen. Pain lanced through my torso.

The few grunts of discomfort I was able to provoke from the ground didn't come close to making up for my own growing agony. And then a sound reached my ears that turned my blood to ice.

The snicker of a switchblade flicking out.

This was definitely more than a warning. If I didn't get my act together, these pricks were going to slit my fucking throat.

Either the men we'd threatened hadn't been scared

enough to act… or Sheeran hadn't given a shit what they had to say about it.

My eyes popped open. I spotted my own knife just a few feet away beyond the deluge of kicking legs. If I could just reach it—

"Get the fuck away from her!"

That voice was familiar. That voice was home.

Rafael barreled into my attackers' midst, colliding with the man who'd been going at my ribs like I was a soccer ball. My bodyguard clenched the asshole's throat hard enough to break the guy's windpipe, hurled him aside, and pummeled three other goons in quick succession.

The distraction gave me all the opening I needed. Gritting my teeth against the pain blazing through my body, I wrenched myself upright and lunged for my knife. With it held tightly in my hand, I jerked around so I was back-to-back with Rafael, glaring at Sheeran's men.

One of Rafael's victims lay on the ground, his head split open from the force of the impact against the corner of the sidewalk. My bodyguard let out a wordless roar, and most of the others took a step back, abruptly a whole lot less confident than when they'd been beating up on a lone woman.

"Two against all of you isn't good enough odds?" I taunted through breaths that felt like fire. "You're not going to try me now?"

Another of the thugs threw himself at me, but Rafael's fist got there first. The crack of a shattering jaw radiated through the night.

When one of his colleagues tried to hurtle past to get

at me, I slashed out with my knife and dragged it through his shoulder. He swore, clapping his hand to the wound.

It still might not have been enough. The other goons were regrouping, massing together to form a solid offensive. I had no idea if Rafael and I could have dispatched all of them.

Then another bellow rang down the street with the thud of racing feet. "What the fuck do you think you're doing to her?"

Two of the men toppled as their heads were bashed together from behind. Jasper shoved into the fray, rage etched on his handsome face, his white teeth bared.

He might have been a figure skater, not a criminal, but he was built as tough as most of Sheeran's guys. And the odds had suddenly swung even more against them, lopsided as they still were.

Jasper got in one more swing before the bunch of them surged backward. "We're not finished with you!" one of them shouted in a dark voice.

They melded back into the shadows of the alley they'd emerged from.

Rafael probably would have given chase, but as he took a step forward, I wobbled and clutched at my side. The pain of my injuries was stabbing at me even more insistently now that my adrenaline rush was ebbing.

Rafael grabbed my arm. "Are you bleeding?" he demanded, his gaze searching my body for injuries.

I shook my head. "Nothing major. A few scrapes. But I think—" I took a strained breath. "I think I've at least bruised a few ribs. Maybe even cracked one." I restrained a wince and caught Jasper's eye. "Where did you come from?"

He stared at me, the anger now drained from his face and replaced with worry. "I finished up the mending that one costume needed and figured I'd walk over to help carry the food. Glad I did. Those were Sheeran's guys? I thought—"

"We obviously weren't convincing enough," Rafael snarled, and then shook himself. "Thank you for jumping in. You didn't need to do that. It helped."

"I wasn't going to just *stand* there." Jasper shifted his attention back to me. "You said they hurt your ribs?"

"Yeah. But I've dealt with that before. No big deal."

I put on a smile that might have been a bit sickly, but as soon as I started walking, the agony lanced through my chest again, making me sway.

Rafael caught my arm. "Take it easy. Come on, I'll carry you."

My dignity wanted me to argue with him, but I had enough brains to realize he was right. As he swept me off my feet into his bulging arms, my eyes caught Jasper's again, and the hint of panic I saw there reverberated into me with a sudden chill.

If I *had* broken a rib, how the hell was I going to perform in two weeks' time?

Sheeran's thugs hadn't succeeded in killing me, but they might have killed my career before it'd even really begun.

TWENTY-THREE

Luciana

THERE WAS nothing on the TV but daytime soaps and talk shows, both of which were full of drama so much more banal than my own life that it bored me to tears.

I groaned in annoyance and slouched on the sofa—and then winced at the flare of pain the movement sent through my ribs. We'd determined they were only bruised, not outright broken, but they still hurt like a mofo less than twenty-four hours after the attack by Sheeran's men.

The ache was a lot duller than it'd been last night, at least. More like a burn than knives being jabbed through my chest.

Niko walked by behind the sofa, stopping to tease his fingers over my hair and press a kiss to the top of my head. "I know you're not good at sitting still, but try to get a little more rest, Angel."

Jasper looked over from where he'd been prepping lunch in the kitchen. "Can I get you anything else? Glass of water, pillow, ice pack?"

The worry in his tone had a slightly frantic edge, which brought a totally different kind of ache to my gut. My guys had been hovering around me ever since I'd made it home, doing whatever they could to ease my pain and keep me comfortable, with no thought for their own needs.

"I'm good," I said. "And I'm coming over to the table to join you for lunch."

Rafael, who was already sitting at said table, stood up abruptly with a scrape of the chair legs. "You stay right there, Lou."

I made a face at him over the back of the sofa and pushed myself to my feet. The burn of the bruising coursed across my torso, but after a few steps I could mostly tune it out.

Not that my stoicism made any difference to the three men. By the time I'd taken those few steps, they'd all rushed to my side.

"You've got to know your limits," Rafael growled.

Niko nodded in emphatic agreement. "If you push yourself too hard, you could injure yourself worse."

I glared at the bunch of them. "I've had bruised ribs before. I know what I can handle. I'm just walking ten feet to the fucking table."

They took my grumbling in stride, helping me over to the nearest chair since they could probably tell it'd be more of a struggle trying to force me back to the sofa.

Jasper set a plate with the turkey sandwich he'd made

for me on the table at my spot. "We wouldn't have minded joining you in the living room. I know you're tough, Punk, but you look like a truck slammed into you."

I grimaced, thinking of the vast purple-brown blotch I'd seen stretching across the side of my chest in the mirror this morning. "It doesn't matter what I look like. No one's going to see through my training clothes—or my costumes."

All three of the men froze in place. Rafael jolted back into action first.

He set one hand on the back of my chair and glowered down at me. "There's no way you should be skating when you're banged up this badly." He raised his head to glance at Niko. "Right? You're the professional—you tell her."

Niko's mouth had tightened. "With an injury like this, I'd never expect a skater to perform. Doctors would recommend a recovery period of at least a few weeks, and then—"

I sputtered a laugh. "Finals is in two weeks, so forget about that."

Jasper reached across the table and grasped my hand. "It's okay, Lou. I'm not going to blame you at all for what happened. Those shitheads fucked us over, and that's on them. You need your time to recover, and then we can take on the competition next year."

I shook my head with a jerk. "No fucking way. I didn't come this far to let some shitty gangsters ruin everything I've been working for. Everything *we've* been working for."

"It's not about 'letting,'" Niko said gently. "The body is only capable of so much."

Jasper let out a wordless growl. "If I'd just gotten there

sooner, maybe they wouldn't have managed to hurt you so badly."

"No sense in beating ourselves up about it." I smiled at him. "Those goons already took care of that for us."

Silence. My joke had landed like a one-winged seagull. All three of them stared at me, incredulous looks on their faces.

"Nothing?" I asked. "Not a single laugh? Come on, we can't sit around moping. We've got work to do. My ribs are bruised, big whoop. I'll rest for another day or two so the worst of the pain has eased off, but then I'm back on the ice, no arguments."

Rafael considered me for a long moment with his best stern expression. "I can't stop you, Lou, but I wish you'd take your basic needs into account more. You know this is the only body you get. If you destroy it, then there's no way you can make skating a career in the long run."

I paused. He had a point.

"I can see a doctor if you guys really want me to," I said. "Just to make sure nothing's worse than it seems. And I'll pick up a cortisone shot to take away the pain so I can practice and perform no problem. Then I can get right back to skating as if none of this ever happened."

Jasper was still frowning. "A cortisone shot? Those things can be dangerous if you're not careful. If you mask your pain chemically and end up hurting yourself more, you could *really* damage your body."

I gritted my teeth. "It's my decision. It's only a couple of weeks before I can take a longer break, and I haven't had a real fall in ages. And, look—I'll be in a hell of a lot more pain if I let these bastards ruin my chances of getting my skating career off the ground."

I paused, glancing around at them, the twist of emotions in my gut rising to join the physical pain in my chest. "I hear what you're saying. I really do. But you don't understand. If I lose this chance… I don't know what's going to happen over the next year. How long I can stay off my mom's radar. Look at how quickly I ended up tangling with two different people who could report my whereabouts back to her. This could be my *last* chance to show what I can do."

Silence fell over the room. Niko and Jasper traded an agonized look.

They all knew I was right. My time with them was precarious. There was no guarantee I'd even make it to Finals without my old life coming crashing down on me, let alone all the way to next year's competitive circuit.

I picked up my sandwich, took a bite, and rallied against those awful thoughts while I chewed. "We do have to get the Harvester's Boston crew off my back before they ruin things even more. Right now, it seems like they're not going to stop coming at me until I give in and leave town. Which is not happening."

Niko's forehead had furrowed. "How are we going to do that? The threats we made didn't work. Are you going to go through with the threats?"

I sighed and swallowed thickly. I'd been hoping I wouldn't have to be part of more destruction. And— "I'm not sure that would actually do us any good. If anything, if we start launching attacks on Sheeran's people, he'll be even more convinced I'm working against him."

Rafael ran a hand over the wiry coils of his hair. "We went after Sheeran's main people before, but not the local boss himself. He calls the shots. We have to find *his* weak spot, something we can use against him."

I rubbed my mouth. "But none of your contacts knew any major dirt on him, right? And you haven't seen anything obvious."

"No. I'll keep at it."

Jasper tapped his fingers against the tabletop and then spoke up cautiously. "There is something… I don't know if it's enough, or anything at all for sure, but it might help."

All our gazes shot to him.

"What?" I demanded.

"From how you described him to us—I think I saw him last night, right before I rushed in to fight those pricks. There was an older guy, pretty slick looking, hanging back by the alley they all ran into when they took off. He was watching the others beat you down."

I perked up. "White hair, dressed in nice clothes?" When Jasper nodded, I did too. "Yep, that'd be him."

Jasper's eyes went momentarily distant in thought. "There was something that struck me, looking at him. The way he had his hands in his coat pockets, the angle of the seams…" He focused on Rafael. "You said that he seems to have an awful lot of money, right? More than you'd normally expect a local gang leader to have unless the main guy he works for was incredibly happy with him?"

Rafael gave the other man a contemplative look. "Yeah, it is pretty extreme. Not saying it isn't possible the Harvester just is that pleased, but it's a lot beyond what I'd normally see. Where are you going with this?"

A smile, nervous but determined, curved Jasper's lips. "I think if we can catch him at the end of one of the business deals he oversees here, we could get exactly what we need."

TWENTY-FOUR

Jasper

I PEERED at the old convenience store where Rafael had determined that Sheeran carried out a lot of his business dealings, just down the street from where we'd paused. The streetlamp overhead buzzed, casting a yellow glow into the darkness of the night. Niko's shoulders bumped against mine with a hint of nervous agitation.

Lou glanced at both of us from beneath the hood of her jacket. "You two don't have to go in with us, you know. I'd *rather* you stayed farther back, someplace safe."

I crossed my arms over my chest, gathering the resolve that'd brought me this far. "Nowhere's really safe until we deal with this asshole. And we're not letting you deal with him alone. Anyway, this was my idea. I should be there."

Niko nodded. "We said we'd stand by you through

whatever danger you faced, and we're not going back on that promise."

Lou sighed but didn't argue. She shifted her weight from one foot to the other as she watched for Rafael's return, no sign of pain in her movements.

She'd gotten the cortisone shot she'd talked about a couple of days ago and today had been skating like she'd never taken a single hit. But I'd seen the thugs who'd come at her the other day. I'd seen how brutally they'd attacked her.

They'd wanted to hurt her way worse than we'd let them get away with. Maybe they'd even have killed her if they'd had the chance.

The idea of losing Lou—at all, but especially in such a vicious, painful way—made my gut clench up. How could I have ever thought *I* had it hard while she'd been dealing with shit like this every day since she was a little kid?

Rafael appeared across the street. He motioned us over to him and led us silently down an alley between the backs of the stores on either side of the block. I set my feet as carefully as I could, understanding that stealth was important.

Niko walked beside me, picking his way nimbly around the bits of trash that scattered the cracked pavement. He caught me looking at him and aimed a quiet smile my way, like a little stream of sunlight through the night.

This had to be done. If the four of us were ever going to live in peace together, we couldn't let Sheeran go any farther in his campaign against Lou.

Rafael held up his hand to stop us again. He moved

forward, melding into the shadows with a skill I couldn't help admiring.

There was a muffled grunt and a rustle of clothes. Then a soft thump.

Rafael reappeared and beckoned us. "Come on, before they notice anything's wrong!"

We hustled past the slumped unconscious bodies of two men I assumed were guards Sheeran had posted, who obviously hadn't expected to encounter anyone like Rafael tonight. My skin tightened at the evidence of his violence, but I marched toward the shop's back door without hesitation.

Sheeran had made the rules here. If he'd left Lou alone, it wouldn't have come to this.

Rafael had taken out a gun that set my nerves even more on edge, though I knew it was for all of our protection. He took just a second to position himself and then threw himself at the door, bursting into the back room.

We barged into the thin artificial lighting to find the guy with the stark white hair I now knew was Sheeran and a few of his underlings standing around a metal table, which held a couple of baggies of a powder I assumed was some kind of drug and a pile of bundled bills set right in front of Sheeran.

He had one bundle in his hand as if counting it, but in the moment we hurtled inside, his other hand was dug deep into the pocket of his wool coat.

He jerked it out as he spun around at our intrusion, but I'd seen enough in the gesture and the angle he'd held his arm at.

I hadn't imagined anything the other evening. All my sewing work over the years had given me a strong sense of seams and clothing construction, and something was up with his pockets. And given everything else we'd discovered about him, I had a pretty clear idea what.

The three guys with him whipped out guns of their own and brandished them at us with threatening shouts. Rafael bared his teeth, positioning himself at the front of our group while Lou flanked him, her knife tight in her hand and her eyes fierce.

"What the fuck is this about?" Sheeran demanded, his jaw clenching as he took us in. He didn't look all that concerned, maybe because his side's guns outnumbered ours, but he definitely wasn't happy about the unexpected visit.

I cleared my throat. "We just wanted to check up on your operation. I was wondering how much money and product you've been skimming off your boss's profits and merchandise. Are your men on board with your disloyalty, or do they have no clue they're helping a backstabber?"

The three gunmen gaped at me, though their weapons hadn't wavered—yet. So, it was door number two, then.

Sheeran's face had hardened into a mask of horrified defiance, panic sparking in his gaze. "I don't know what the fuck you're—"

"Oh, it'll be pretty easy to prove it," I interrupted, stepping forward as if those guns didn't have my heart thumping double time. "Should we give these guys a show so they know who they're actually working under? Maybe it'd be a nice step up for them in the ranks, huh, if they could tip off the man at the top of the ladder about what his trusted lieutenant has been getting up to behind his back."

"They're making shit up," Sheeran snapped. "Shoot them already!"

Rafael fixed our enemies with a cool stare. "They know that's not a good idea. I can take down at least two of them before they could manage to stop me. Pretty poor odds, and for what? To support a traitor?"

"And we can prove we're not making anything up." I tipped my head toward his coat. "Your pockets will tell the whole story, won't they?"

The thugs glanced from us to Sheeran, looking increasingly uncertain. The fact that Sheeran had paled at my words couldn't have helped their confidence in their boss.

The older man appeared to make a hasty decision. He jerked his hand toward one of the thugs. "Give me that."

When the guy handed over his gun, Sheeran waved for them to go out the back door. "I can take care of this bunch. You make sure no other idiots are skulking around, looking to hassle us."

"But—" one of the gunmen started to say.

Sheeran glared at him. "Get the fuck out and follow your orders, or you'll be getting a bullet in the skull too."

Rafael waved at them with his pistol. "Go right ahead. I won't stop you."

Frowning, the three men filed out into the back alley. Lou positioned herself by the door so she'd hear their return.

She narrowed her eyes at Sheeran. "If you think you can cover up what you've been doing, *you're* the idiot. No matter what your men here know or believe, I can call up the Harvester directly and tell him the score."

Sheeran scoffed, though his knuckles had whitened where he gripped the gun. "You can't prove anything."

I raised my eyebrows. "Oh, no? You'll need to explain why you've got custom secret pockets stitched into this coat—and who knows how many other pieces of clothing. And why he'd find traces of the ink used on cash and maybe drugs as well in them. That stuff wouldn't wash out easily."

"We wouldn't give you a chance to try anyway." Lou smirked at him. "I could make the call while we have our little standoff, and I bet he could have someone checking your house in an hour or two, no sweat."

No sweat for the Harvester, anyway. A few beads of perspiration had formed on Sheeran's forehead. "You fucking bitch," he snarled.

She shrugged. "Look, I don't even care how you're screwing over your boss. Do whatever the hell you want… as long as you leave *me* out of it. I've told you before and I'll tell you again: I don't give a shit about your territory. I'm only here to skate. I've cut all ties with the Deadly Rose. I'm not a threat, and all I want is for you to leave me alone."

Sheeran snorted. "The Deadly Rose's heir wouldn't simply run off to take up figure skating. You might as well try to sell me on the story that you've joined the circus."

"How would you know?" Lou retorted. "You don't know a thing about me. Just because my mom pushed me out of her body doesn't mean I'm her carbon copy. I'm capable of wanting different things from this oh-so-fantastic life." She motioned around her at the dingy room.

"You have access to so much more than this. No one throws that away—not the power or the money."

"Speak for yourself, jackass."

Sheeran's lips curled into a sneer. We'd had him on the defensive, but now he was mocking Lou again. The possibility that she was telling the truth was so far outside the realm of what he could imagine that he hadn't even bothered to look into her story. Or maybe he figured she was spending all that time in the arena as a front for some criminal scheme.

My heart sank. Even this gambit wasn't going to work... because I didn't think Lou did have an immediate line to any members of the Devil's Dozen. Not without her mother finding out and ruining everything anyway.

So how the hell could we—

A spark of an idea drew me up short. We could *make* him look.

I turned to Niko. "You have some recordings of our latest run-throughs of the routines on your phone, right?"

Niko blinked at me. "Of course."

I made an urgent gesture toward the bulge of the device at his hip. "Show this dickwad what she can actually do. What no one who hadn't dedicated themselves to years of skating practice could possibly pull off."

Without needing any further prompting, Niko whipped out his phone. As his thumb darted across the screen, Lou shuffled her feet, her stance tensing. "*No one's seen the full routine except us.*"

I glanced at her. "We've got to convince him, right?"

Sheeran was rolling his eyes. "If you think a little video of her gliding around a rink is going to make a difference—I'm not an imbecile."

Niko ignored his comments, turning the phone's screen toward him. The familiar melody of our free skate music pealed from the speakers.

I knew the movements of the routine by heart, on or off the ice. With each beat, my muscles flexed instinctively, the motions playing out in my head. I didn't need to see the video to follow what it showed.

The wavering light played across Sheeran's grim features. He adjusted his grip on his gun, his sneer deepening. "Very nice. You set up this whole farce to pretend—"

His voice fell away with the swell of the music—the moment when we'd launched into our first synchronized jumps. The first lift would be next, Lou spinning over my head and stretching into a pose so graceful you'd think she was not just an angel but a goddess incarnate.

Watching her enemy take in her performance, Lou grimaced but didn't try to intervene. I couldn't imagine she liked him seeing this part of her life, the part she'd carved out through so much effort from the past he represented. But it'd been the only way I could think of to solidify our case.

Sheeran had tipped forward just slightly, his gaze now glued to the screen. The sneer was fading from his face. At the next set of jumps, a sequence hard for even pros to pull off, his eyes widened.

He was bull-headed but not stupid. He could tell there

was no way Lou had simply picked up those moves in a few days' practice.

Niko watched the other man's face. His voice came out quiet but firm. "*This* is what Lou is in Boston for. It's the only reason she's here. She doesn't have time to worry about your criminal activities while she's training for the competitions."

I lifted my chin. "It's taken her years of practicing every day since she was a kid to reach that level. A lot of people *never* get there, no matter how hard they work at it. Are you so much of an imbecile that you think she did all that just to sell a cover story one day? A cover story no one in your line of work would believe anyway?"

Sheeran's lips parted at the lift-throw sequence we'd been working on so painstakingly. He shook his head, but not in denial, only as if trying to sort out his thoughts.

"I—" Sheeran yanked his eyes away from the screen with apparent effort. He looked at me and then Lou with a dazed expression before his shoulders came up slightly with a hint of shame.

"It *did* sound ludicrous," he said grouchily. "And I was specifically told otherwise—that you were here on a mission for the Deadly Rose."

Rafael hummed to himself. "Let me guess. Your tip came from a pale guy with a big nose and acne scars. Maybe you even dug enough to find out his last name is Haggard?"

Sheeran's attention snapped to him. "How did you know that?"

"That prick used to work for the Deadly Rose. *Used to* being the important part of that sentence. He's got a vendetta against her and everyone associated with her. He was only trying to stir up trouble for Lou for his own gain, and you bought into it hook, line, and sinker."

Sheeran grimaced. "What was I supposed to think? His version made a lot more sense than hers."

I glared at him. "Well, now you know. So, you'll pass on word to your boss that she isn't a threat and leave her alone from now on, right?"

Lou piped up before Sheeran had to answer. "We're going to take care of Haggard, so you don't need to worry about him. And if you back off on me, we'll leave all the Harvester's business and your own reputation alone. I'm sure you've got better things to do than keep track of what I'm up to anyway. Seems like a pretty sweet offer."

To my surprise, Sheeran looked back at the video still playing on Niko's phone before answering. He watched me and Lou whip through our final sequence with bewilderment in his eyes.

As Niko tucked the phone away, the gang boss inclined his head to Lou. "Fine. I can see I made a mistake, and I'll fix that as long as we're even. Consider it a done deal."

TWENTY-FIVE

Luciana

ONE PAIR of our competitors spun across the ice in their free skate routine, creating an image I could appreciate even as my stomach knotted with apprehension. I rested my hands against the boards, resisting the urge to fidget.

In some ways it was a good thing that Finals were being held in Boston this year, so we'd been able to stay in the same city and perform in an arena we were familiar with. But when I glanced around the vast space, I couldn't help flashing back to our qualifying competition performance.

The jolt of panic that'd raced through me. The wobbles and stumbles.

The shame of hearing our score and knowing it might not be good enough.

Jasper and I had performed our short routine yesterday without any significant errors, but the caliber of the competition was much higher at Finals. All the best pairs from across the country were here, and we'd only ranked fifth.

That was okay. We both knew that the free skate was where we really shone, and with the adjustments we'd made, it'd earn us all the points we needed to boost us up the ranks. It counted for twice as much of the total, after all.

As long as we didn't screw it up. As long as *I* didn't fuck it up.

We had to make it into at least the top three to be sure of getting accepted into the National Championships, the stepping stone to the international circuit. If we failed here, it'd be nothing but minor local competitions until the qualifying round started again next year.

I can do this. I just have to keep my cool, and I'll nail it.

The music wound down. The skaters struck their ending pose, bowed, and glided over to the stands.

There were still a couple more pairs to go before it was my and Jasper's turn, but my stomach clenched even tighter. This was going to be our first time showing off our new move in front of any audience. And a faint ache still radiated through my ribs despite the cortisone.

I'd rest some more, for at least a few days, after we got through today. That was a promise to myself.

But I still had to get through today.

A hand rested on my shoulder with a gentle squeeze I recognized before I'd even glanced up at Niko. My coach shot me his sunbeam of a smile, pride shining from his face as if we'd already proven ourselves.

"You're going to kill it, Angel," he said. "Both of you. Show them what you can do, and let them experience the beauty you have to offer the world."

I inhaled slowly, absorbing those words. He was right: my purpose was to add beauty to the world, not take from it. All I had to do was remember who I was—who I *truly* was, not who Mom had wanted me to be—and I would be golden.

I shot Niko a smile in return. "Thanks. I'm ready. It's just hard not to be a little nervous."

He gave a light laugh. "I don't think you'd be human if you weren't. But I've seen you face off against a lot more than a bunch of ice. I know you can do this."

The corners of my lips twitched higher. He wasn't wrong about that either.

My gaze drifted away—and caught on a set of bright blue eyes fixed on me from farther down the stands. My pulse skipped a beat, but I forced myself to continue my survey of the stands as if I hadn't even noticed Quentin's stare.

He'd been watching us—watching *me*—almost every time I'd glanced in his direction since we'd shown up for Finals yesterday. I couldn't tell whether the intensity of his attention was more unnerving or thrilling.

Was he trying to intimidate us? Hoping to rub his and Jess's third place spot after yesterday's routines in our faces?

Having trouble shaking the images from the night when he'd spied on us in the locker room?

I hoped it was the latter. Let him keep stewing on the

passion he knew we shared, that he and his partner had no chance of matching.

Whatever the case, I wasn't going to let the jerk distract me.

As the pair on the ice launched into a jump that wasn't quite as impressive as our triple Lutzes, Jasper stepped up beside me. He stared out over the ice with a solemn expression that sent a pang through my chest.

He had to be nervous too. This was his grand return after his slump—and I'd already almost ruined it for him.

Had Niko and I really done the right thing, dragging him back into the spotlight? I didn't even know everything that was weighing on him.

I reached out and tucked my hand around his. "Jasper?"

His gray-green eyes slid to meet mine, warming as they did in a way that reassured me. "Yeah, Punk?"

I couldn't hold back a grin at the teasing nickname, even though it was still a little hard to get out the question I wanted to ask. "We never really talked about… about whatever it was that got you off track the last time you were competing. I know it wasn't because of Niko. Is there anything you're still worrying about?"

Jasper blinked, and then his gaze went momentarily distant. "Oh. That. I—I mean, it's mostly the same old thing, just it happened to hit me really hard at a time when I really needed my focus."

He rubbed the back of his neck in his awkward way, and I resigned myself to the fact that he might not say anything more. But then he caught my gaze again. "I've told you that my dad wasn't supportive about the whole figure skating thing."

I nodded. "Yeah. He sounds like a total jerk."

Jasper let out a rough chuckle. "That's one way of putting it. Well, a couple years ago, he and my mom took in the teenage son of friends of theirs—the parents had a great opportunity with work that was taking them overseas for a few months, and they didn't want to pull the kid out of school in the middle of the year. So he was living with my parents for the time being."

"That was nice of them," I said, wondering where this was going.

"It was." His jaw tightened, and he returned his attention to the ice. "The kid was on his high school football team, star quarterback, already getting interest from colleges even though he was only a sophomore. I went back home to visit for a few days around Easter, and my dad just wouldn't stop going on about how amazing this guy was, how impressive this game or that play had been, with little jabs implying *I* was a total letdown in comparison."

My hands balled at my sides. "Not just a jerk. A total fucking asshole."

Jasper shrugged. "I always knew he felt that way about skating. He just hadn't had such an easy point of comparison right there in front of him before to rub it in. That wasn't even the worst of it. My mom got upset with him, and the night before I left, they had a blow-up argument, yelling like they hardly ever did. And he stormed out of the house. He hadn't come back when I had to leave to catch my flight the next morning."

Good riddance, I wanted to say, but I suspected that comment wouldn't come across as all that helpful. "I'm glad you have someone who'd stand up for you."

"I guess there's that. But she still loves him even though he has that one hang-up. I could tell she was devastated. And then I went out and started practicing, and had a few bad stumbles, and all these doubts rose up about whether everything I'd been doing really was worth it. I got too much in my head, like Niko always says. Even worse when the pressure was on during the actual competitions."

Jasper paused and squeezed my hand. "I didn't know how to get back out of that spiral until the two of you showed up. I know *I* was an ass to you when we first met, but you have no idea how happy I am that you tolerated it enough to stick around while I got my head on straight."

A glow of affection lit in my chest. I bobbed up to give him a quick kiss. "I'm awfully happy I did too."

While we'd talked, the pair right before us had gone on. They were just wrapping up their routine, but as I watched them strike their ending pose, I found my own niggling doubts had waned.

Jasper and I really had created something special, and there was nothing I wanted more than to show it off in all its glory for the audience around us.

The announcer called out our names, and Jasper tugged me toward the ice. We skated into the middle of the rink.

Jasper aimed one more smile at me. "Okay, Punk. Let's show them how it's done."

As we assumed our opening position, I felt like I was

made for this moment. The audience went silent, all their attention on Jasper and me.

Then, at the back of the arena among the logos for the event's various sponsors, a new banner unfurled before my eyes. A white sheet with red paint blazoned across it in the shape of a broken rose.

The picture was crude but unmistakable. My heart lurched.

It had to be Haggard's doing. He'd set up that banner here to taunt me—he was *here*, in the arena, probably right now to watch my reaction.

Through the flare of panic, my jaw set. Niko's words about how much I'd faced off against came back to me.

My men and I had overcome an entire crew of Devil's Dozen people. If this one psycho thought he was going to faze me, he was delusional as well.

The chill of fear melted in the wake of my anger—and a renewed surge of determination.

The music swept through the arena, and Jasper and I launched ourselves into motion.

The music carried us as if we were propelled by an ocean current. I caught Jasper's gaze as we whirled around each other and saw the same fierce certainty in his expression that'd steadied me.

He was in this to win just as much as I was. We had each other, and nothing was going to hold us back.

The melody flowed through me, and the routine became a blur. Jump, spin, lift. Every motion perfectly timed, the two of us in sync as if we had one body.

The poignant joy of the song wound through me and

lifted my spirits. I let it play out in every tiny gesture of my hands while it shone in my face.

This was what skating was all about. We were spreading that joy to the hundreds of watching figures in the stands, transporting them to another place of our design.

Then it was time for the new combination.

Jasper's hands grasped mine. I whipped into the air over his head, finding my balance in his hold without a single wobble. The faces around us raced by with our rotation, and the music buoyed me even higher.

When Jasper propelled me up a second time, I whirled around with a sensation of perfect freedom. The air seemed to hold me up as my body spun, and my foot hit the ice at the perfect angle as if drawn by a magnet.

As my skates hissed across the rink with my landing, triumph swelled in my chest. Applause and cheers echoed from all around us. I had to hold back a victorious grin that wouldn't quite have matched the mood we were still trying to convey.

Take that, everyone who'd ever thought they could steal this moment away from me.

We swept through the rest of the routine hitting every mark and struck our ending pose with the last note of the song in one final dramatic touch. The roar of the crowd washed over us, and I finally released my grin.

Jasper beamed back at me, clasping my hand and thrusting it higher over our heads before we gave a quick bow.

As we skated back to the stands, my pulse thrummed in my veins. Niko grabbed us both in a hug, and shouts of congratulations carried from the seats around us. The energy coursing through the crowd after our performance exhilarated me.

But nothing mattered unless the judges had gotten caught up in our performance too. Had we done enough? Had they seen everything we'd meant to conjure with the routine?

The announcer took the scoresheet they handed over. He paused before leaning toward the mic, and my heart almost stopped.

"The score for Luna Garcia and Jasper St. Pierre is one hundred thirty-six point two seven."

Another thunderous cheer rose up through the stands. My jaw dropped.

We'd gotten over a hundred and thirty-five points? Even a hundred and thirty was rare. Holy shit.

My world spun. Jasper let out a startled crow of amazement and wrapped me in a hug. Niko flung his arms around both of us, and in that moment, there was nothing in my entire being but joy.

TWENTY-SIX

Luciana

BY THE TIME Jasper and I were called onto the ice for our second-place finish—our amazing free skate score tugged a bit low by our not-quite-as-spectacular short program—the giddy rush of excitement hadn't faded. I didn't stop grinning once as we stood side by side, basking in another round of applause.

Somewhere in the stands, Quentin and Jess would be watching. Their performance a couple of spots after ours had looked not just precise but rigid to my eyes, and Jess had lost her balance during one of the lifts, nearly kneeing Quentin in the face as she fell.

Despite their solid showing in the short program, they'd dropped down to seventh. I might have grinned even wider knowing that this was the last we'd have to see their smug faces around, since there was pretty much no chance they'd be welcomed at the National Championships with that placing.

Sure, I might miss the competitive thrill of facing off with our rivals a little, but it'd be more than worth it not to have to see Jasper's frustration when that jerk mouthed off at him.

It was hard to believe I'd made it this far when just months ago, I'd thought I'd never be able to compete at all. I resisted the urge to pinch myself.

I kept my arm looped around Jasper's waist as we skated back to the stands. When we reached Niko, I pulled him into yet another hug before aiming my grin at both of them.

"This is the best day ever. Obviously we need to celebrate. I'll run and get changed—then we can figure out where to go for dinner. I'm ready to pig out!"

Niko laughed and gave my cheek a quick kiss. We all tramped off toward the locker rooms.

The woman's room was crowded with my fellow skaters peeling off their costumes. As I eased out of mine, careful of Jasper's painstaking needlework, several of the other women came over to congratulate me on the performance.

"I can't wait to see what you and Jasper do at Nationals!" one of them, who I thought had placed toward the bottom of the pack, said with an eager smile.

I let out an awkward laugh, not used to having the attention focused on me. "Me too! Thank you."

I threw on my old Metallica shirt and a pair of faded jeans, restraining a wince at the slightly sharper ache of my ribs when I raised my arms. I had pushed myself pretty hard in the last couple of weeks—it was definitely time for some resting before we honed our skills for Nationals.

After I tucked my costume into my equipment bag, pausing to brush my fingers over my lucky skate lace from my earliest childhood lessons, I raised my head and noticed a door off beyond a row of lockers along the wall. It was narrower than the main entrance and scuffed. Probably for maintenance or something.

But what caught my eye was the smear of red paint just above the handle.

My pulse hitched. I froze for a second, my gaze darting around the room, but none of the other skaters appeared to have noticed it, let alone started worrying about it. Several were already taking off through the main door, eager to get home after a long, stressful day.

But I knew Haggard had been here. He'd left that broken rose banner for me to see.

What was he playing at now?

Simply ignoring the sign didn't feel like an option. I couldn't turn my back on an enemy without figuring out his new game.

I hefted my equipment bag and walked casually over to the side door. Setting the heavy bag down on the nearest bench, I gave the door a gentle tug.

It wasn't locked. When I peered out into the dim hall on the other side, a part of the arena that clearly wasn't generally open to the public, the streak of paint continued along the wall farther than I could see.

A shiver ran down my back, and my teeth set on edge. I was *not* letting Haggard fuck up the best day of my life.

I also wasn't going to throw caution to the wind. I

pulled out my phone, tapped a hasty text to Rafael to let him know what I'd found and what I was doing, asking him to catch up with me as soon as he could.

I wasn't sure how he'd get into this hall while avoiding the woman's locker room, but this was Rafael. He'd find a way.

After putting my phone away, I reached for the knife in my other pocket. Holding it ready, I treaded slowly but steadily down the dim maintenance hall, following the trail of red paint. Splatters of it marked the floor as well, still gleaming wet.

A few other doors broke the sameness of the pale gray wall. I was just passing one when a hushed voice reached my ears, as if from someone standing right on the other side of it.

It was Quentin's voice.

I paused automatically, my ears pricking. As I leaned closer to the door, I made out the words of what sounded like one side of a phone conversation.

Quentin's tone stayed low and a little hoarse. "I'm sorry. I don't know what happened. It was fine when we practiced— Yes. Yes, I know that. Of course Jess and I tried our best. No, you can't blame it all on her. I was just — Mom, it wasn't like that. I still have another chance. I'll do better, I promise."

An uneasy twinge ran through my gut. This didn't sound like the arrogant prick I knew at all, but someone brow-beaten into submission.

I was way too familiar with having those kinds of conversations with my mother. Who'd have thought Quentin had a shitty one too?

Maybe that was where he'd gotten his shitty attitude from. I squared my shoulders and pushed myself onward.

I had bigger things to worry about. Our rival's family situation didn't even make the top ten.

I edged down the hall, stifling another shiver. The red blotches on the floor grew larger with every step I took. The smear on the wall continued on to a bend several feet ahead, where one more puddle of paint seeped around the corner.

I hesitated, inhaling the stale air and wishing Rafael had made it here already. My fingers tightened around my knife.

For all I knew, Haggard was already gone. Laughing to himself about how he'd freaked me out yet again. I'd just get to the end of the trail, see what was what, and then I could shut him out of my mind at least for tonight.

I pushed myself forward, my eyes peeled, alert for any hint of a threat. But I still wasn't totally prepared.

The second I edged past the bend in the hall, a gangly body in a denim jacket hurtled into me. As my attacker tackled me to the floor, a blade flashed in his hand.

The side of my skull slammed into the linoleum floor. I thrashed against the man's hold, my thoughts spinning with adrenaline and pain, and caught a glimpse of a hooked nose and a cruel mouth I recognized even in my daze as Haggard's.

He snatched at my wrists, brandishing his knife with his other hand. "I'm going to paint the place with your blood next, Cordova bitch!" he snarled, his spit flecking my cheek.

I shoved at him, squirming away from him with all my

might, and the swipe of his blade only nicked a shallow line in my forearm. With a growl of frustration, he heaved me toward the floor again.

I'd gotten my torso briefly free, but he had my legs pinned beneath the weight of his body. Even as I flailed, I couldn't unseat him to aim a knee at his balls or any other vulnerable area that might have turned the tables.

So I did the best I could with my upper body. Ignoring the swipe of his blade, I jabbed at his chest with my own knife. When he smacked my arm to the side, he gave me the opening to punch him hard in the nose.

Haggard grunted and clamped his hand around my throat. "Fucking cunt. You deserve everything that's coming to you! You're a stuck-up, stupid whore, just like your mother."

Just like your mother. Those words echoed in my ears, sparking a blaze of denial that reverberated through me like a battle cry.

I was *nothing* like Mom, and I'd proved it out there just hours ago. I'd proved it despite this psycho's best attempts at shattering my confidence.

I hadn't let him win then, and I sure as hell wasn't about to roll over now.

Rage flared inside my chest. This prick had been hurling so much shit at me, messing up my life and dragging everyone I cared about into that mess, just to get back at someone I had no association with anymore.

I was nothing like Mireya Cordova, but I was still her daughter, with all the lessons that had come with the role. I would do whatever it took to end this sicko's campaign of terror.

With a renewed surge of strength, I wrenched to the side, just as Haggard stabbed at me again. His blade pricked my shoulder, but I rocked his balance. As he swayed, I rammed my elbow into his gut.

Haggard's breath spurted out of him in a pained huff. Anger twisted his features. He jerked around to pin me more solidly again, but I was already whipping up my hand at the perfect angle.

I grabbed his wrist with my other hand, yanking it down to clear the way, heedless of the scratch his knife drew along the side of my bicep. With all my strength, I jabbed my knife into the side of his neck.

It plunged in all the way to the hilt. Haggard's lips parted with a gurgle; blood splattered from the wound down over my chest.

As his body crumpled, I scrambled out from under it. My back banged into a pair of legs that had just jarred to a stop behind me.

I almost struck out before a big, brawny form dropped down to encircle me in his arms. Rafael held me tight and glowered over my shoulder at the slumped body spilling its life blood across the dingy floor.

I stayed frozen for a few more beats of my heart until Haggard's corpse sagged with total limpness. There wasn't a single sign of life left in him, not even a twitch of his fingers.

Rafael tucked his head over mine, his stance taut with tension.

"Are you okay?" he asked, his voice terse with strain. "That cabrón—"

I dragged in a long breath. "I dealt with him. I'm fine."

Only as I spoke did it sink in how true those words were. Not the slightest quiver of guilt or regret rose up at the sight of the man I'd murdered.

I raised my chin defiantly. "The world is better off without this prick. I did what I had to do to make sure it wasn't me lying there in a puddle of blood."

Rafael hugged me tighter for a moment and pressed a kiss to the top of my head. "You did fucking amazing, Lou. Both out there on the ice and right now. The bastard got everything he deserved. But maybe next time, wait until I'm there for backup."

I grimaced. "I didn't really expect to find him. He's never stuck around before."

A hint of wryness crept into my bodyguard's tone. "And he never will again. Let's get you cleaned up to go back to your celebrating. I can handle the mess back here. Somehow I don't think this asshole is going to be missed."

"You've got that right."

I pushed myself upright, standing next to Rafael as he checked over my minor wounds. My nose wrinkled at the metallic scent now lacing the air, but I didn't let myself look away from the man I'd killed.

He *had* deserved it. And now the world had one less psycho in it. My *life* had one less psycho in it.

I might not want to resort to my mother's bloody methods, but I'd done what was necessary. Come what may, no matter how far I tried to leave my past behind, I had to hold on to a little of what I'd learned.

I could never let myself get so afraid to turn to violence that I'd falter when it was truly the only answer.

TWENTY-SEVEN

Luciana

BY THE TIME Rafael and I emerged into the main hallway to meet Niko and Jasper, the full impact of what had just happened hit me.

I'd been ambushed by my lunatic stalker. He'd nearly *killed* me.

His blood was still clinging to my skin on the tee I'd covered up with a hoodie from the equipment bag Rafael had surreptitiously retrieved for me.

None of the blood or my minor wounds was showing, but Jasper took one look at me and frowned. "Are you okay, Lou? What happened?"

"I'm fine," I said, managing a smile that I could feel came out tight. "I just…"

As I trailed off, momentarily lost for words, Rafael stepped in. Ducking his head and lowering his voice, he must have conveyed the gist of what I'd just been through to the other two men.

Niko's eyes widened with a stiffening of his shoulders, and rage flashed in Jasper's eyes, but Rafael gripped the younger guy's shoulder.

"I'm going to take care of everything else. Lou will be okay—it was just a lot."

I shook myself out of my daze. "Yeah. And it's over now. So let's get on with the celebrating!" I aimed a steadier smile at my men. "I want to enjoy what we pulled off here today and forget about the assholes we've had to tackle. There's no one I want to think about other than the three of you."

A whiff of the bloody odor reached my nose, and I wrinkled it before adding, "And we should definitely go back to the apartment first, because I have some washing up to do."

Niko patted his phone in his pocket. "I've gotten a few calls, media enquiries and a possible new sponsor, but I already put them off until we had a chance to regroup. That can wait until at least tomorrow."

My bodyguard gave me a quick kiss and disappeared back into the maintenance hallway to take care of the body. Just this once, I was grateful for the connection Rafael and I shared with the criminal underground—it meant that he knew how to make problems like this disappear without a trace.

I let Niko drive and stretched out in the plush backseat. When we got home, I ditched the bloody shirt and dragged my sore and soiled body into the bathroom to start the shower running.

"You sure you don't need any help, Angel?" Niko asked, concern etched across his handsome features. "I don't mind if you need to lean on me."

"I'm good. I'll let you know if I'm feeling wonky. But I think I'm feeling more like ordering in than going out for dinner now. Why don't you two figure out something delicious for us to chow down on?"

When I stepped under the hot spray and inhaled a lungful of soothing steam, the last of the adrenaline rush faded away. I let out a relieved sigh.

Haggard was gone, and Sheeran was out of my hair. We'd skated to victory today, and we had every hope of reaching greater heights in the future. And now no one else was left to interfere.

I scrubbed my skin until it shone golden-brown, as though I could wash away the events of the day down the drain with the crimson-tinted water. By the time I left behind my steamy heaven, Rafael had returned. He passed me on his way into the bathroom to wash up himself, giving me a nod to signify that the deed was done.

I never had to even think about Haggard again.

The smell of fresh, cheese-laden pizza reached my nose from the dining area, setting my mouth watering. It might not be the most elegant of meals, but my men obviously knew me well. Next to pierogies, nothing said comfort like a big, greasy slice of pie.

As I headed over, something else reached me that was totally unexpected. A high feminine voice carried through the air. "Jasper, you both did so well. It was amazing to watch! I just wish I could have seen it live instead of just a video."

My eyebrows shot up. "Is that Emi?"

Niko beamed and motioned me over to where he was holding his phone so both he and Jasper could video-chat with his sister.

Emi waved from the small screen with both hands, grinning avidly at me. "There you are!" she cried. "Congratulations, a hundred times. I'm so proud of you, but then again, I just knew you two would come out on top."

Her eager words swept away any lingering tension from the day. My heart swelled with affection totally different from what I felt for my men but no less poignant.

I waved back with a grin of my own. "Thank you! I wish you could have been there too. We worked our butts off to give that performance."

She laughed. "And the judges must have noticed that! It was the best part of my day—no, my whole week. Now you get back to your dinner. I have to hurry to work."

As Jasper popped open the two pizza boxes so I could take my pick, Niko tucked away his phone and headed for his bedroom. "I have a little surprise to go with the celebration!"

He returned with a bottle of champagne—with a label that told me it'd been a pricy purchase. My lips parted in surprise as he dug out the cork with a satisfying *pop*.

"You must have bought that before the competition. We didn't stop anywhere on the way home."

Niko's eyes sparkled as he poured the bubbly liquid into the glasses that'd come with the apartment. "I had a suspicion that we'd find a good use for it sooner rather than later."

A rush of warmth flooded my chest all over again, and I only held myself back from jumping on him with another hug because that would have meant champagne splattering all over the place.

Rafael joined us, claiming a slice and a glass. I dug into my perfectly tangy meat-lover's and gazed around at the makeshift family that'd somehow formed around me.

My bodyguard offered a reserved but clearly amused response to one of Niko's enthusiastic remarks. Jasper had stepped closer to our coach, his shoulder brushing Niko's, with a comfortable companionableness that made me giddy. When he caught me watching, his smile was only a little sheepish, full of all the same fondness wound around my heart.

This was all the family I needed. It seemed like a miracle that we'd come together at all.

Rafael and I had figured out how to navigate the figure skating world, and Niko and Jasper were now holding their own against criminals. We'd met each other halfway and created something so much stronger out of our differences.

I polished off a second slice of pizza and washed it down with a healthy portion of champagne. The bubbles set off a headier exhilaration through my veins.

I was hungry for something better than food.

Setting down my glass with a forceful clink got all the guys' attention. My lips curled into a sly smirk.

"There are other ways I want to celebrate."

Without waiting for their response, I stepped toward

Niko, who happened to be closest, and pulled him to me. He dipped his head to meet my lips, his mouth opening instinctively to allow my tongue entrance.

As he hummed his approval into my mouth, hands came to rest on my waist from behind. Jasper tipped his chin over my shoulder to kiss the crook of my jaw. "I think we've already proven we can collaborate on that kind of celebration *very* well."

I reached up to stroke my fingers down his face and then eased to the side so the two men could steal a kiss from each other. The growing confidence with which Jasper gripped the collar of Niko's shirt and angled his head to deepen the kiss sent a flush of heat through me that was both joy and desire.

But there was one other participant in our celebration —one whose reaction I was much less sure of. As Niko and Jasper drew apart, Jasper nuzzling my hair and Niko trailing his hand down my side, I glanced over at Rafael.

When I'd first met the skaters, he hadn't liked the idea of me hooking up with them at all. He'd admitted that he found it hard to accept sharing me. We'd gotten this far by keeping the most explicit parts of our relationship away from his watchful eyes.

But if there was a slight flicker of jealousy in his gaze as he stared at me now, it was barely visible amid the flare of lust.

"I'm not letting these two have all the fun," he rumbled in answer to my unspoken question, and stepped in to capture my mouth with his.

I tilted my head up to lean into the demand of his kiss, letting out a ragged sound when his fingers skimmed down my torso to squeeze my ass through my leggings. His free hand found its way into my hair and twined itself in the strands with a domineering grip.

He yanked my head back with just enough force to set my nerves singing, not the slightest prick of real pain. "You think you can handle three at once, huh, brat?"

I gave him my best bratty smile. "I know I can. The question is, can you handle me?"

He chuckled with a hint of promise that left me tingling from head to toe. "Oh, I'll make sure you're satisfied, all right."

Jasper raised an eyebrow. "I think we're all going to contribute to that."

Rafael's eyes smoldered. "Sure you will. Why don't you start by giving the side of her neck some attention? I hope you know how sensitive she is right at the crook of her shoulder."

The bossiness in his tone combined with his total confidence about what I'd like set me on fire. Even more so when Jasper followed his order, pressing scorching kisses down my neck and then nipping the crook with the edges of his teeth.

A gasp spilled out of me, and I ground my ass against him instinctively. Jasper let out a groan of his own at the friction I'd generated.

Niko smiled mischievously and curled his fingers around the hem of my shirt to lift it.

Rafael nodded approvingly. "Nice and slow. Tease her all the way up."

Oh, God. I didn't think I'd ever been so turned on in my life. My panties were soaking, and none of the men had even touched me below the waist other than Rafael's brief ass squeeze.

Niko eased my shirt up just as Rafael had directed, stroking his fingertips over my belly and then my breasts through my sports bra. My breath caught when he flicked them over my nipples, raising them to peaks simultaneously.

Jasper gave him room to peel the shirt right off me and grasped my bra in turn. He slid his hands under the fabric to cup my breasts, massaging them and swiveling his thumbs over the nipples. I swayed with the pleasure racing through my chest.

Niko turned to Jasper next. The other man went still for a second before raising his arms to let Niko strip his own tee off him. Our coach took the same teasing approach, drawing a flush across Jasper's chest that spread up his neck to his cheeks with Niko's playful caress.

Seeing their attraction to each other only fanned my own desire hotter. I wrenched at Rafael's shirt, determined to get as much delicious musculature on display as I had within reach.

Time slowed with a blur of stroking hands and hot mouths. More clothes tumbled onto the floor until we ended up kneeling together on the living room rug, stark naked.

I ran my fingers down Rafael's six pack to the jut of his impressive cock, and he growled. Without giving me a chance to do more than circle it with my fingers, he pushed me down on the rug.

"You," he said in the commanding voice that had me

shivering with pleasure. "Get down there between her knees and give her what she deserves."

What I deserved?

His meaning became clear an instant later with Jasper's head bowing so it was sandwiched between my thighs. My partner's tongue darted out to lap over my clit and then lower to devour my entire pussy.

I keened and shuddered, rocking into his eager mouth. Jasper grasped my ass and tipped me up so he could work me over even more thoroughly. I melted against his lips and tongue.

Rafael's voice came out raw. "Good. Just like that. And you, take care of those tits."

Niko offered a light chuckle. "Nothing I'd rather do."

His slender hands palmed my breasts. As he pinched my pebbled nipples, sparking jolts of bliss, a full moan reverberated out of me.

Rafael wasn't leaving himself out. He eased toward me, tangling his fingers in my hair again, but all my attention was on the thick shaft between his legs. Carried on the waves of delight rushing through my body, I lifted my head and flicked my tongue over the tip of his cock.

Rafael gave a shudder of his own with a groan that made my pulse skip. I wanted to taste him, to take him all the way down my throat.

At first I thought he might pull back, but then he growled and slid forward. I took every inch, bit by bit, sliding my tongue along his shaft. My hand reached out to rake my nails against his bare thighs.

"A huevo!" he muttered, pumping toward my mouth. "So fucking good, Lou."

Niko lowered his head to suck one nipple between his lips, and my cry reverberated over Rafael's cock. He let out a ragged breath and pulled back, just as Jasper grazed his teeth over my clit.

I moaned again, but it wasn't enough for Rafael. Twin fires glowed in his dark eyes. "I say we fill her up properly. Are you ready to take a ride, brat?"

I licked my lips, but if he thought I'd turn right to him, it wasn't going to be that easy. As Jasper raised his head to take in the shift in the situation, I pushed Niko over on his back and straddled him. Then I shot a grin at Rafael. "Sure am."

Rafael didn't look at all put out—and Niko definitely wasn't. He slid his cock against my pussy with a worshipful sigh.

"You need—" Jasper scrambled away and returned moments later with a condom packet.

Niko's eyes shone as he watched the other man. "You want to prepare me for her?"

Jasper hesitated, but only for a split-second. His teeth grazed his lower lip in the most delicious way as he ripped open the packet and reached to roll the contents over Niko's cock. He delved his fingers into my wetness at the same time, taking my arousal as lubrication.

Holy hell. Lust gripped me, and I sank down onto Niko. He slid right into my slick channel, filling me all the way to the sweet spot deep within.

Niko groaned softly. "You always feel so good, Angel."

"You too," I murmured, bracing myself against the rug. I began to rock my hips against him, my tits bouncing with every thrust, welcoming him even deeper.

As we moaned in unison, his eyelids fluttered—and his gaze slid to Jasper, who'd planted himself beside me to return his attentions to my neck and breasts. Carefully, Niko lifted his hand and trailed it over Jasper's thigh. The top at first, and then easing inward in time with the rhythmic collision of our bodies.

Even through the pleasure hazing my mind, I couldn't help tracking the movement. Jasper paused, watching as if hypnotized.

Niko grazed Jasper's rigid shaft with the tips of his fingers, gazing up at the other man. Jasper closed his eyes, his throat working.

As far as I knew, they'd never gone quite this far with each other before, other than the brief help in "preparation" Jasper had offered a few minutes ago. Niko's caution seemed to confirm my suspicion.

The silent question hung in the air, and then Jasper nodded, opening his eyes with a blaze in his grey-green irises. Niko smiled.

His chest hitched as he plunged into me once more, and he wrapped his hand right around Jasper's cock. With a swipe of his thumb, he smeared the beading precum down Jasper's length and began pumping him as he pushed up to meet me.

Jasper's eyes rolled back. "Christ, keep doing that."

Niko did as he was told, his smile lingering on his lips. Jasper's breath stuttered, and he buried his face in the crook of my neck again, passing on some of the pleasure the other man was provoking in him.

Just when I thought the thrill inside me couldn't surge any higher, I felt a third touch at the small of my back.

Rafael had positioned himself over Niko's legs behind me. He teased his fingers farther down, parting my ass cheeks and tracing the rim of my back entrance.

His voice spilled hot down my spine. "Would you like to be ridden at the same time, Lou?"

All I could manage to work from my throat was a strangled sound of encouragement. I felt Rafael's smirk in the press of his lips against my shoulder blade. Then there was a clicking sound.

When his fingers returned to my ass, they were slick with lubricant. I didn't know when he'd gotten it or how he'd anticipated this moment, but I sure as hell wasn't complaining.

Rafael worked one finger inside me and then another, provoking a different but equally heady burn of penetration. As he stretched me, readying me for his thick cock, I started panting.

The bliss rippling through me had already brought me to the brink. But I wasn't going to give myself over to it until I'd felt everything my men had to offer.

At the first nudge of his cock against my back entrance, I bit back a whimper. It turned into a giddy gasp as he slid in ever so slowly, swaying with Niko's motions beneath me. I slowed, allowing him to take me until he was balls deep and my whole body rang out with the pleasure of it.

Then we all started moving again, gradually gaining speed as we found our harmony with each other. The roar of pleasure drowned out every sensation other than the ecstasy roiling through me.

Jasper slipped his hand between me and Niko to

massage my clit, and the extra jolt of delight made me determined to pay him back just as much. I arched over with a tug at his hips, urging him into a position where I could join Niko's efforts.

My tongue lapped over the head of his cock, and Jasper groaned. I let it slide between my lips with every vigorous stroke of Niko's hand.

A guttural sound resounded from Jasper's chest. "Fuck, that's amazing. Oh, fuck. I'm going to…"

The rasped words were enough of a warning, but I had no intention of pulling back. I reveled in the spurt of his cum into my mouth.

Rafael grunted behind me, driving into me with all the force I loved, while Niko pounded my pussy like it was his last day on earth. I tried to stretch out the bliss a little longer, but my self-control careened away from me.

I cried out my climax to the ceiling, quaking between my men, clutching on to them as I soared over the edge. Stars sparked behind my hazed eyes.

My orgasm caught Niko up in its impact. He groaned, and his cock pulsed wildly inside of me. He slowed his thrusting as he poured out his own release.

Rafael was not so easily won over. He looped an arm along my stomach and increased his pace. I worked my body against him, giving him everything he gave me. As he gripped my hips with both hands and let out a roar that set my skin quivering, I came again on the heels of my first climax.

We sagged together in a jumble of naked limbs. I hummed happily, totally sated. "Now all I need is a joint cuddle under the covers."

Rafael let out a peal of laughter. "You're going to need to get a bigger bed," he said. "Make room for all of us to fit."

Like he was already imagining the four of us tucked together on one mattress. Like he *wanted* that.

A grin stretched across my face with the almost unbearable happiness that we'd all come to accept our strange relationship. "I bet that could be arranged."

TWENTY-EIGHT

Luciana

I WOKE up early the next morning feeling parched but otherwise content. Despite my current bed only being a normal-sized queen, my three men had managed to squeeze onto it around me anyway. The heat of their bodies surrounded me, along with Rafael's soft snores and Jasper's and Niko's drowsy breaths.

For a moment, I just lay there, luxuriating in the sense of love and companionship unlike any I'd ever known before. But my throat kept panging with its demand for hydration, and my bladder twinged too.

Grimacing, I eased myself out from between the three sleeping men and managed to slip off the bed without waking any of them.

On my way out of the bedroom, I grabbed my phone, but Emi hadn't sent any new texts overnight. Sometimes she forgot that we were on totally opposite daylight schedules with her on the other side of the world.

I tucked the phone into the pocket of my pajama shorts, made a quick stop in the bathroom, and then ambled over to the kitchen to pour myself a glass of water from the faucet. Leaning against the counter in the faint dawn light, I took a few slow gulps until the itch of thirst retreated.

I was just setting the glass down, planning to clamber back into my manly nest on the bed, when my phone chimed after all.

My lips twitched into a smile, anticipating a barrage of emojis, but when I glanced at the screen, my body tensed.

The number wasn't anyone in my contacts, but the message made it clear enough who'd sent it.

Hey. It's Quentin. I need to talk to you.

I raised an eyebrow at the implicit demand. Maybe *I* needed to never see his stupid if admittedly striking face again. I debated ignoring him but then decided I might as well figure out what he wanted.

How did you even get my number? I wrote back.

Registration records are a thing, you know. And not exactly top secret. Can you come down? I'd rather talk in person. I'm outside your building.

Both of my eyebrows shot upward at that last sentence. *You tracked down my address? Stalker much?*

It was also in the registration records. No big deal. Are you going to come down or what?

Still an asshole, even to the end. I blew at my bangs in exasperation, but in spite of my snarky remark about stalkers, I didn't think I'd just picked up a new one. I'd never gotten a dangerous vibe from Quentin, only a jerky one. Over the years under my mother's rule, I'd gotten lots of practice at telling the difference.

That didn't mean I wanted to chat with the guy, though.

As I hesitated, the phone chimed with a follow-up text. One that said simply, *Please?*

Huh. Exactly how much pride had that single word cost Quentin's massive ego?

I shifted my weight from one foot to the other. What could he possibly want to say to me that was so important?

Whatever it was, if I didn't go along with his request right now, chances seemed good that he'd hassle me when Jasper was around—and possibly hassle Jasper too. I'd rather spare my skating partner the frustration of dealing with his rival if I could.

And I couldn't deny that I was a tiny bit curious too.

Fine, I typed with jabs of my thumbs. *Give me a minute.*

I pulled on a hoodie over my tank top and shorts, both to cover me up and for the comfort of my knife in the hoodie's pocket. Just in case my instincts were wrong. After shoving my feet into my sneakers, I trotted down the stairs to the lobby.

Quentin was standing just outside the glass front door. His shoulders were slightly slouched, but he straightened up when he saw me coming with a glint of what might have been *relief* in his piercing blue eyes.

As I stepped out onto the sidewalk, he drew back to make room for me. No one else was around at this early hour, the sidewalks empty, only a single car puttering past while I frowned at the uninvited visitor with my hands shoved in my pockets.

Quentin swiped his hand over his hair, which was looking unusually rumpled, a few strands falling free from the slicked-back 'do. He glanced at the sidewalk and then back at me as if he didn't know what to say. As if he wasn't the one who'd called me out here.

"Well?" I said, raising my chin. "What's going on? What are you dragging me down here in the middle of the night for?"

Even now, he couldn't restrain that arrogant smirk. "Technically it's the early morning."

I glowered at him. "Who the fuck cares about the details? Everyone's asleep. What's so important it couldn't wait until after breakfast?"

His jaw worked. "I was hoping I could see you without St. Pierre as your shadow."

"Here I am. Are you going to get on with telling me what you want?"

Quentin cocked his head. "What if I just wanted to see you?"

"Seriously?" I let out a scoffing sound and spun on my heel toward the apartment entrance. "That's not even a real reason."

Before I could take a single step, Quentin's hand shot out. He caught me by the upper arm and whirled me around faster than I could have anticipated to push me against the wall next to the door. He leaned close, his arms caging me in.

He hadn't yanked me hard enough to hurt, but my

temper flared anyway. In an instant, my knife was in my hand, the blade aimed at Quentin's chest.

My heart thumped away, an electric buzz passing through my nerves as Quentin glanced down at the knife and then back at me with a faintly amused expression. Not that I'd ever admit it, but something about his complete disregard for the obvious threat turned me on.

"I'm not done," he said, his voice low and taut with an intensity that quivered over my skin. "I was going to tell you that I'm going back to Singles. I can still compete at Nationals that way thanks to my placement last year."

My jaw clenched before I managed to speak through my annoyance. "And I should care because…?"

He smiled with a flash of his white teeth. "I'll admit that you and Jasper beat me, but I think it's mostly you. The way you skate…" He paused, the intensity in his eyes searing brighter as he held my gaze. "I haven't been able to stop thinking about you. You've gotten into my head, and I can't get you out."

The previous quiver turned into a full out tingle, sweeping through my body against my will. I ignored the unwelcome reaction and scowled at Quentin. "That sounds like a you problem, not a me problem."

"Hmm, I wonder." He leaned even closer to me, his head bowing close enough that his breath grazed my cheek. "You knew I was there that night, didn't you? I could tell when you realized. Did you like knowing I was watching you take both of them in the locker room? Did it get you off?"

My face flushed, and I gritted my teeth, at least as

pissed off because I *had* gotten off on the knowledge as because he'd brought it up.

I gave him an insistent shove, tapping the blade of my knife against his shirt. "Back the fuck off, Quentin."

"Not yet," he murmured, and then he slammed his mouth into mine.

The kiss hit me with a jolt of surprise, irritation… and a little thrill. Quentin claimed my lips with a determination that reverberated through my body in the fleeting second before he pulled himself away, just as I was about to shove him harder.

He stepped farther back, tucking his hands in his pockets. "We'll talk more later."

As the words rang in my ears like a promise, he turned and stalked off without waiting for an answer.

I wiped the back of my hand across my mouth, annoyed all over again at the shiver of heat that passed through me at the memory of the kiss. For fuck's sake, I didn't want anything like that with Quentin Wolfe, of all people. Hotness didn't trump assholery.

What the hell had gotten into him? I'd thought all he cared about was seeing Jasper—and therefore me—crash and burn. Now suddenly he wanted to strike up a relationship?

No, this was probably about Jasper too. Just a different way of trying to one-up his rival. He could forget about using me to accomplish that goal.

I peeled myself off the brick wall with a little shake. As I gathered my composure, a dark sedan cruised up to park on the other side of the street, directly opposite me.

A twang of alarm I couldn't explain resonated through my bones. I tensed, turning to dash into the lobby—

And the car door opened to reveal an all-too-familiar form, emerging from within to stand on the asphalt.

My legs locked. I stared, not quite able to believe what I was seeing. My heart pounded like a jackhammer.

My mother glided across the street with measured steps, raising her hand to hold it out to me.

"Almost as if you were waiting for me. How perfect. You've had your fun, Luciana. Now it's time to come home."

ABOUT THE AUTHORS

Eva Chance is a pen name for contemporary romance written by Amazon top 100 bestselling author Eva Chase. If you love gritty romance, dominant men, and fierce women who never have to choose, look no further.

Eva lives in Canada with her family. She loves stories both swoony and supernatural, and strong women and the men who appreciate them.

Connect with Eva online:
www.evachase.com
eva@evachase.com

Harlow King is a long-time fan of all things dark, edgy, and steamy. She can't wait to share her contemporary reverse harem stories.